THE
GLAMOUR
THIEVES

DON ALLMON

D1550842

RIPTIDE
PUBLISHING

Riptide Publishing
PO Box 1537
Burnsville, NC 28714
www.riptidepublishing.com

The Glamour Thieves
Copyright © 2017 by Don Allmon

Cover art: Simoné, dreamarian.com
Editor: Sarah Lyons
Layout: L.C. Chase, lcchase.com/design.htm

ISBN: 978-1-62649-616-3

First edition
August, 2017

Also available in ebook:
ISBN: 978-1-62649-615-6

THE
GLAMOUR
THIEVES

DON ALLMON

RIPTIDE
PUBLISHING

To Barb

THE GLAMOUR THIEVES

Chapter 1 1

Chapter 2 13

Chapter 3 19

Chapter 4 29

Chapter 5 33

Chapter 6 45

Chapter 7 57

Chapter 8 71

Chapter 9 85

Chapter 10 97

Chapter 11 113

Chapter 12 127

Epilogue 139

CHAPTER ONE

A ustin Shea was wearing the same damn Sanzi wraparound sunglasses and blue-and-green-flowered Hawaiian shirt he'd been wearing the last time JT had seen him. The same khaki pants, tight through the crotch and thighs, loose through the legs. Same shoeless feet like he was a druid and couldn't lose touch with the ground without losing his power, which was almost true.

Austin took the sunglasses off, and his eyes glittered under the Arizona sky like gold-flecked emeralds. He let the glasses dangle from his fingers as he draped his arms over the winged-open door of the Corvette Dawnstrike FX27. He cocked his head and smiled his winning smile, lopsided. That meant he was about to lie his ass off.

"Hey, JT," he said. "Been a while. Nice place ya got here."

JT's place: The yard was filled with recyclable scrap plastics and metals like it was a junkyard. The work sheds were prefab, and all of it was surrounded by a turreted wall that made the place look like a prison. There were a dozen urban-support vehicles all lined up in a row being prepped for shipping. Four-legged robots the size of Great Danes crawled among them, polishing. The air smelled of paint and desert heat.

JT folded his arms. "*My* place makes *you* trespassing. Get off my land."

The smile didn't let up. "I missed ya. You're looking good."

JT's looks: Baggy overalls covered in axle grease and transmission fluid. Plastic baseball cap stained with six years of sweat that smashed his Mohawked hair down and made his green ears stick out even more than usual. He hadn't shaved in four days.

JT nodded at the car. "Who'd you steal that from?"

"I didn't ask his name."

"I'm calling the police."

"Fine. Go ahead. Christ. I can't even say hi."

They both turned away simultaneously, like they were reverse images of each other—an expression of frustration one had learned from the other, and who could say which one had done it first?

Neither of them moved. JT didn't call the police.

The Corvette was a coupe on the old design. It was painted Event Horizon Black, same color they were using these days for stealth tech. Illegal in Pacifica. The car was rumored to get six hundred KPH on the magway, plenty of speed to make paste of yourself if you made a mistake. It was an off-balance kind of car, took the right touch to drive—a better touch than Austin had. It took a touch like JT had.

Just knowing that car was there, not even having to see it, made JT's blood pump a little bit faster. Seeing it, yeah, JT went a little hard. And no, none of that had anything to do with Austin standing there, hair too long and falling over his eyes, long knife-ears swept back and pale in the sun, long, hard-muscled arm draped over the upturned wing of the open door. And thank god for baggy overalls, or Austin might have seen JT hard—might have thought it was him JT was hard for and gotten all kinds of wrongheaded ideas. It was the car, JT told himself. Only the car.

"You can't bribe me with a stolen car, Austin."

"Ain't no need."

"Because whatever it is, I'm not doing it."

"Don't want nothing, JT," Austin said, the damned liar.

JT rubbed his hands on his coveralls, except now they were just as filthy as his hands, so he stripped out of them and left them lying there on the pavement, blue jeans and a Nochi'iru Kitty T-shirt underneath. He touched the fender of the car the same way old Catholics touched statues of the Virgin Mary, except there was nothing virgin about this car here.

JT circled around, and Austin circled around like they needed to keep the car between them. And maybe they did. JT slid into the driver's seat, and Austin slid into the passenger's side. The seat molded to JT's broader frame and shorter legs, and still the cabin was a bit cramped. Had he been any bigger, he wouldn't have fit. They never sized the nice cars for orc bodies. Orcs never got anything nice.

Austin said, "It's unlocked."

JT tapped the wireless key and initiated the handshake between his neurals and the car's brain. "How did you even steal this thing? This is state-of-the-art. You shouldn't have gotten five blocks without a police lockdown."

"I'm not helpless."

"How'd you do it?"

Austin ignored him, evasive as always.

Controls passed to JT's neurals, and his senses bled into the car's nav array. High-end as this array was, it took less than a second for the additional senses to integrate, all sliding together like oiled glass. He let out a shaky sigh. His sense of self slipped, a bit of vertigo, and now the car and his body were all one thing. He could feel the car's engine the same way he could feel his own heartbeat. The dash lit with hologram displays. JT didn't need them, but not many people had the built-in tech to the extent he had.

Austin jutted his chin out. "You aren't going to comment on my beard?" What Austin called a "beard" was a patch of short dark peach fuzz on the point of his chin. It tapered out along the edge of his jaw.

"How long did it take you to grow?" JT kept it icy because he sure as hell didn't want Austin thinking this car was going to work on him.

"Two years. Started it right after you left."

"I suppose it just grew in like that. Didn't have to trim it or shape it or anything."

"Well, yes."

JT shook his head. "Fucking elves."

"You're bound and determined not to pay me a compliment. You know I said you were looking good. Second thing I said to you."

"But not the first thing. You don't need me to stroke your ego."

"Returning a compliment, it's only polite."

"Fine. You look like an elf. You're gorgeous. Same as every other elf."

"I'm going to pretend you meant that sincerely. Thank you. I've been working out." Austin flexed a biceps, rock-hard and scar covered.

"You have not."

"No, I haven't. It's all genetic." He looked out the window. "So I fucked a guy until he fell in love with me and gave me the code to his car."

"I don't believe that."

"It's true. I'm a very good fuck."

"I ain't fucking you."

"I ain't this, I ain't that—that's all I'm hearing from you. When did you get so negative?"

JT laid his heavy hands on the dash and sighed. "What do you want?"

"I want you to drive this car. The way it's supposed to be driven, not the half-assed way I drive it."

JT threw the Corvette into gear using nothing but his mind—that and the quarter million dollars' worth of electronics inside his skull and down his spine. They coasted the lane that led to the highway, JT getting used to the touchy controls. It was like waking from a cramped sleep, all your limbs numb and not working like they should, overshooting some marks and undershooting others, and a growing tingle that was almost painful, neural pathways forged and opening. And slowly, slowly, the tingle went away and you remembered, *Oh, this is how you walk.*

He opened a channel to Dante and said aloud, "Dante, goin' out for a bit. Keep an eye on the place."

"Gotcha, boss," came Dante's voice back. "Who's that you're with?"

"No one important." JT cut the signal.

"Girlfriend?" Austin teased.

JT rolled his eyes at the thought. "Apprentice."

"You're teaching her how to steal cars?"

"Teaching her how to build them."

"An apprentice. How old-fashioned and responsible of you."

"I got a business, Austin. A good business. A legitimate business. I got investors. Important people with a shitload of cash and two shitloads of influence. I don't need that old life anymore. I'm done with it."

"And yet here you are with me in a stolen car. It would be just like old times if you were wearing a few less clothes."

They pulled onto the magway. It was a black expanse a hundred meters wide, stretching east to west until it vanished over the horizon. Embedded beneath the surface of the tarmac was a series of focused electromagnets, the whole thing nothing more than twelve magnetic bobsled channels running side to side. Theoretically safe as daisies.

JT flipped the mag array and tucked his wheels up, bouncing a bit as the two fields settled against each other. His heart was thumping hard and fast, knowing what was coming. "Ready?"

"Born."

"We'll see about that."

For several seconds the car crept forward as if nothing had happened. Coriolis drift.

JT acquired twenty new senses he hadn't had fifteen minutes ago: radar, gravimetrics, magnetic fields down to the planetary, weight distribution and balance because he was centimeters off the ground and now moving at one hundred KPH so smoothly probably Austin didn't even know that. One bad dip to the side and it would throw them out of the mag-channel.

Finally, acceleration you could feel. One hundred fifty. Two hundred. One G and the memory foam was resetting, adding lumbar support, pushing back.

Look at Austin. Austin's nose with that break at the bridge; those long, swept-back ears he was so bitchy about back when JT would try to bite them; lips, slightly parted, goddess, those lips; that chin with its stupid peach-fuzz beard and how would that feel rubbed on JT's balls? Austin's head was pressed back into the seat, and he was grinning and panting like he was getting sucked off on a roller coaster ride.

Three hundred KPH. Four hundred. Five.

JT could feel the pressure all the way through him, all the way from tip to tailfin. He could feel wind pass over his sleek plastic body. It hugged him and circled him. There was no reason for pressure sensors on the surface of the car except to let the driver feel the sliding grip of the air. And he was fully hard now and probably leaking, it felt that good. This was what you got in a car that cost over one million: you got a car like sex.

Outside in the distance ran a herd of horses the Apache had reintroduced, racing the car. Austin cheered them on. He was whooping and shouting and shaking his head. His feet pounded the floorboard. JT couldn't help but smile and let go a long, satisfied growl, Austin's joy infectious. They were both of them kids again, both of them stupid. This was how to run: six hundred KPH and ten centimeters of air between you and dying. And this infectious joy, this was Austin's glamour all over again, reaching out to JT, stroking him with memories of how it once had been. Once upon a time, something like this would have left them wrestling in the seats to see who went down on the other while the world outside flashed by.

Back when JT was a car thief and Austin an asshole more than anything else (which honestly wasn't much different than today), and Grayson and Roan were still living, Bell Anderson had sent them all out with a case of beer and a dime of weed to get to know each other better. She wanted her new team to have a sense of camaraderie, she'd said.

Three hours later and they'd been parked on the top floor of a San Francisco parking garage having a picnic at 3 a.m. JT and Austin were lying in the bed of the truck, beer bottles in hand, looking up where there should have been stars but the city lights made the sky nothing. Some gala-something or maybe a prison break swept a spotlight over the sky, and their eyes tracked that like it was something interesting. Roan and Grayson were going at it in the cab hard enough to make the truck rock sometimes. Roan was Austin's sister, but he didn't seem to mind he could hear her fucking. He'd laugh when the rocking got too frantic and the empties in the truck bed rolled around. JT eventually worked up the nerve to laugh along with him, and that took some of the tension out of the air.

And only because he was drunk, JT had said, "Don't you got any self-respect at all?"

"Generally, I find it gets in my way. Is there something specific you don't like about me?"

"The bow-and-arrow thing. Don't you think a bow is a bit stereotypical? Don't you think we got enough problems without people looking at you and saying, 'Oh look, elves really do carry bows'?"

"I'm better with that bow than most people are with a gun. And let me tell you, there's the stereotype and then there's me doing the stereotype, because when I'm doing it, people forget they ever seen it before, that's how goddamn good I am." He mimed drawing a bow, aimed at a spotlighted cloud, and snapped his fingers open. He looked perplexed that the light didn't go out. "You wanna talk stereotypes, let's talk stereotypes. Is it true orc vaginas got teeth?"

"That's an urban legend, not a stereotype."

"That's an evasion, not an answer."

"How am I supposed to know? When have I ever seen one?"

"You've seen one."

"Not up close for real."

"Not even just being curious?"

"And how am I supposed to do that? ''Scuse me, can I see your vagina? It's okay; it's for science'?" He took a swig of beer. "I heard elf jizz tastes like cotton candy."

"It does. Mine tastes like strawberries. Better than orc jizz. Orc jizz is green and tastes like old toilet water."

"Is that what they say?"

"That's what I know. I've fucked an orc before."

"Bullshit."

"It's the first thing they tell you. Don't fuck orcs. They're just as likely to kill you as get you off. Contusions. Ruptured spleens—"

JT snorted.

"I'm serious. So first thing we all do, of course, is fuck us an orc. Just the once. And then we know better, firsthand. Green toilet jizz."

"No elf's ever fucked me," JT said, as if that was evidence Austin was lying.

"Maybe that's because you're ass ugly." Austin hiked himself up on his side and set his nose only centimeters away from JT's. He swayed a little, drunkenly, his eyes glittering as if they caught light from somewhere, but JT knew it was just a trick of the elf's glamour.

Austin's breath was warm and smelled sour from beer. He had a drunken mischievous smile, so goddess-blessed pretty in a haphazard, hard-edged way, with his tousled black hair and a once-broken nose. Annoying how an elf could take a broken nose and make it perfect. But that was the glamour too, wasn't it, because JT liked broken-up men.

"So what did he do to you?" JT asked.

"Who?"

"This orc you fucked."

"The first one? Broke two ribs." Austin was only a centimeter away now, whispering, each consonant a puff of breath on JT's lips, and JT was pressed as hard into the bed of the truck as he could have been, cornered like he was afraid of this beautiful man.

"Really?"

"Yeah." Austin's eyes changed color, the gold expanding. "And then he made me come."

"Shit," JT said, entranced.

Austin closed his eyes, and his lips brushed JT's, soft and hot as a fever. He ran his tongue along JT's lower lip, turned his head and brushed his cheek across JT's stubby tusks, sucking at them, left and right. "So what are you going to break?"

Acceleration like coming: lasting forever and over too soon. Only six seconds and the 'Vette topped out at six twelve. Probably JT could nudge it further. If a polarity switch mistimed and they spun out, he could probably recover. So he pushed it up, KPH by KPH, all his senses hyper-tuned to the transmission spin and the quantum-timed switching, in a zone-like sexual thrill, ready to respond to the slightest bit of stutter. How long had it been since he'd piloted such a beautiful machine? Since he'd taken an apprentice? And then the unwanted thought: what if Dante pulled some stunt like this?

Well, shit.

He eased the acceleration. They coasted along, the ride so smooth and the land outside so flat, it would have barely seemed like they were moving at all if it wasn't for wind slick over him like warm oil. Yeah, six twenty-six would do just fine.

JT adjusted himself, the pinching too uncomfortable to ignore. Austin watched him shift his junk around, grinning that sly, sleepy grin he had when he was horny. "I could do that for ya."

"We got traffic coming up."

"Computer can handle it."

"Don't think I don't know what you're doing."

"Is it working?"

Well, of course it was working. Goddess, Austin was beautiful. Two years, and JT had forgotten how beautiful Austin was, and JT's half hard-on went to three-quarters and was pinching again.

They hit traffic, and JT slipped through it, hopping magnetic lanes like a boat hopped waves, a small stomach-lurching thrill each time. The car swung and bobbed, and vehicles flashed around them and disappeared. But all JT's and Austin's attention was on each other.

"Why don't you tell me what this is all about?" JT said.

"Sex."

"No, it isn't."

"Really, this isn't working?" Austin cast an analytical glance to JT's crotch. "Because it looks to me like this is working."

"It's not working enough."

"Christ, a hot car, me, how much more do you want?" Austin huffed, sat back, and looked out the window. "I need to borrow a few drones."

"No. What for? No."

"I'll pick 'What for?'"

"I meant no."

"For a good cause."

"How much money turns something into a 'good cause'?"

"This job ain't about money. Look, I'll buy them from you. This car for some drones."

"This car's stolen. And you can't pilot drones anyway."

"Oh, you're right!" Austin snapped his fingers with mock realization. "So I'll need you too."

"No."

"I thought we'd moved past negativity and had a bonding moment here. Tell me this doesn't feel good, letting go a little? Tell me you don't want to know what it's like to have sex in this car at six hundred kilometers per hour?"

What would it be like? JT would last about half a second before he nutted all over the leather seats, that's what it would be like. JT said nothing, not trusting himself to say what he should.

"Fine," Austin said. "I have a protection job. Not just a bodyguard walk-around-and-look-mean kind of thing: a serious protection job."

"I'll put you in touch with Duke. He runs a merc outfit in Greentown. You can hire—"

"This ain't a merc kind of job. It's an Austin-and-JT kind of job."

"You mean it's illegal."

"I mean it's for a friend."

All our friends are dead, is what JT wanted to say, but the two of them had managed to make it an hour without any mention of Roan, Grayson, Bell, or the lab job, and he'd be damned if he was going to start now. "What friend?"

"Buzz Howdy."

JT first saw Buzz Howdy in the winter of '70. Roan had run with two gangs: Bell Anderson's team along with Austin, Grayson, and JT; and a group of hackers called 3djinn. 3djinn had been mostly anonymous foreign handles except for Buzz Howdy, who'd been an SF local and Roan's roommate for a while. JT and Austin had been parked curbside at Roan's Mission flat. As she climbed into the truck, she'd waved up at the second floor of the Edwardian and there he was in the window: a shaggy-cut redhead, cute as can be.

"Boyfriend?" JT asked her.

"Buzz? Just a friend."

"He's cute."

"He's brilliant. He's also quiet and nice and you wouldn't like him."

"I like quiet and nice."

"No, you don't." She'd shot a pointed glance at her brother in the backseat, evidence to the contrary.

"What's he do?"

"He forges identities for people who want to be someone they aren't."

"He's cute." JT smiled up at the guy, as friendly as he could, because you never know, some day. The guy saw all those teeth bared at him and drew the curtain.

"Buzz is harmless. Who's after him?" JT said.

"The Electric Dragon Triad."

And that was a death sentence. It seemed unfair, and the news hit harder than he'd expected, twisting his stomach. He tried to hide it as best as he could because Austin didn't know anything about him and Buzz, did he? And he didn't *want* Austin to know. The elf would just tease him. "Buzz is as good as dead."

"Just me alone? Yeah, he would be. But you and me both? We can get him out of town."

They coasted a while more, and JT finally turned off the external sensors that let him feel the wind on the car. He flipped the car's magnetic breaks and jumped a few channels to the outside track.

"We turning around? Is that a yes?"

Did he and Buzz count as friends anymore? It didn't really matter. He owed Buzz for this life. And here was his chance to apologize for that kiss.

"Don't make me regret this, Austin."

CHAPTER TWO

"**Y**ou can't go," Dante said. "We got a meeting with Suborbital on Friday. Duke has been working on getting us in the door for months. You can't ditch it just to run off with that . . . that . . . that . . . *elf*."

Austin had gone into the house, a one-story bunker of a building, and JT had gone to break the news to Dante. He'd found the kid in the lab programming the industrial 3-D printer. The control booth for the printer looked like it could have launched the Mars missions: eight 210-centimeter monitors in banks, holo projectors glowing blue, sim receivers, interface gloves and crowns, and cabling everywhere, all mounted on a half-cylindrical frame of matte-black carbon alloy and plastered with skate-punk decals. The decals were Dante's contribution to the decor. She'd even found an antique Misfits one somewhere.

JT said, "The meeting's two days from now. It's just San Francisco. I'll be back in plenty of time."

"We have a meeting with the banker tomorrow."

"You can handle it."

"Are you insane? Caldwell ain't gonna take me seriously. I'm seventeen!"

Seventeen going on forty, JT thought.

Four months after JT had arrived in Greentown, Dante Riggs had caught his eye. The kid had been looking at JT's truck the way JT had once looked at trucks: paying too much attention to security systems, sight lines to the driver's-side door, and surveillance cameras.

Two days later, she tried to steal it. Duke's boys had beaten the hell out of her, but JT wouldn't let them call the cops. Honor among thieves, he supposed. And damned if the kid didn't come limping back, except this time she wanted to talk: "They tell me you built that truck from scratch," she'd said, eyes still bruised and one tusk broken off short. "3-D printers and nano shit. Teach me how to do it."

"Fuck off," JT had told her, and hit her again so she understood he was serious.

JT said now, "You're just reviewing affidavits for Friday. You're not asking him for money. You'll be fine."

"I don't own a tie."

"Caldwell wouldn't recognize you if you wore one."

"He's going to fuck up your life again!"

Ah, there it was. Out of everyone JT had met since he'd moved here, he'd only told Dante the truth. It wasn't the business Dante was worried about—it was Austin. Well, that made two of them. "It's only one day, and it's only this once."

"Yeah, I've said that about a lot of things too."

"And so have I. But I got things to come back to this time."

After JT had told the kid to fuck off, Dante had camped out at the gate to JT's place like she was petitioning for training at a Shaolin Temple. JT had managed to hold out a week before he brought the kid in.

JT clapped her on the shoulder. "I'll be back, I promise."

The kid worried her broken tusk with her tongue—everyone learned their habits from someone—shoved her hands deep in her pockets, and hunched her shoulders like eighty degrees was cold. "Yeah . . . well . . . when you come back, lose the elf." She looked out across the yard at the black space where the Corvette sat. "But keep the car."

Kitchen, dining and living rooms were all the one room. On the dining table, Chinese takeout was unpacked, white boxes everywhere like blown-up origami. Austin had opened everything to make sure there was no meat in his, and he'd arranged the too-many packets of soy and duck sauce in letters: *EAT ME*.

He was on the couch, and the big-screen was going at the same time he had the VR glasses on. He absentmindedly worked chopsticks on vegetable lo mein. He didn't even look at the damn box or have to readjust the sticks every minute like JT had to. He never dropped a bit of it or had to fish around to find something easy to pick up. That was his left hand.

His right hand flicked and twitched in the control glove, and Nazi zombies died.

"Are you cheating?" JT asked.

"I only cheat in real life, when it's actually fun. The kid not eating?" He ate and killed zombies.

"Nah, she's eating by herself tonight." He'd set Dante up in a room over the printer lab when the kid had moved in, and Dante retreated there when she needed her space or JT needed his.

"Tonight? But doesn't she eat with you usually?" Austin asked, implying something, but JT didn't want to play games, so ignored him. JT speared orange chicken with his chopsticks. The container of rice sat untouched. Rice was elf food. "She could be useful," Austin said. "Maybe—"

"Maybe nothing. I brought her here to give her a way out of that life, Austin, not a way in."

Austin turned just a bit and slid the glasses down his nose (and still his hand flicked, and zombies died, and he didn't), and ran his eyes up and down JT. "You make a cute daddy. I approve."

"Fuck you. I'm just doing what I can."

"You didn't have to do anything," He went back to his game and his food. "That's what makes it cute."

JT started in on the Szechuan chicken, upending the take-away box to his mouth and using the sticks to shovel the food in. He watched Austin play his game and eat.

"Shouldn't we be planning this protection job?" JT asked.

"What's to plan? We need to move Buzz from the place he's holed up in San Fran to Tahoe and his rendezvous with 3djinn. The quieter, the better."

"Route? Gear?"

"You're the pilot. As far as gear, I'm bringing a bow, some arrows, and you. Really, JT, this isn't a break-in. It's just deliver-the-package.

Except the package is Buzz. Pick a car; pick your drones; and we're good to go."

That was just too much blitheness, even for Austin. This was a triad they were messing with, not some street gang. Something was up.

"So what's the story? Why's the triad after Buzz?"

Austin shrugged. "He stole something."

"Software?"

"Something. I don't know. He calls me—"

"He's got your contact info?" JT didn't even have Austin's contact info.

"It's not that hard to find." He gave JT a pointed flick of a glance. "If you wanted to find it. So he calls me and says he's in trouble and needs to get out of town and over to Tahoe. He'd been working for the Electric Dragon Triad and found something, and, well, he might have taken it—"

"So he didn't just steal from them, he betrayed them?"

"Suppose you could see it that way."

"I can guaran-fuckin-tee you that's how they're seeing it." The Electric Dragon was going to be excessive in their vengeance. But it was like Austin had said: they just needed to move Buzz quiet, not a shot fired. "So he never said what it was he took? Must have been something pretty damn amazing to throw your life away for it."

"Must have been." Austin stopped playing his game and took the VR glasses off. "Things like that exist, JT."

"Like hell, they do. And you still don't think we need a plan."

"I got a plan. You."

Hours later, drones all folded up sleeping in the truck bed, software all loaded, and fuel cells charged, JT came back into the house. Austin was still up, still plugged into the VR, but doing what JT couldn't tell.

JT crossed to his bedroom door. "I'm getting some sleep. You can crash on the couch. I'll get you some blankets."

Austin took the glasses off. "What's wrong with your room?"

JT had known this was coming. "Floor's a little hard in my room." He didn't crack a smile or make a friendly joke of it. Dante had been right, and JT couldn't risk getting tied up with Austin again. JT had to draw a line, and that line was at his bedroom door.

Austin looked away and worked his mouth as he stared at the ceiling. He looked back and said, deadpan, "Hey, no worries. I'll find a motel."

JT didn't watch him leave, not with his eyes. But every camera networked into his head tracked Austin, one camera after another. They tracked him as he stalked out of the living room, door banging closed behind him. Tracked him across the gravel yard and concrete slabs. Tracked him sliding into the stolen Corvette and spinning it around faster than he needed so the wheels sprayed up gravel. Tracked him, taillights red, down the road toward Greentown, and then kept watching the road after the taillights had been swallowed up by the night.

CHAPTER THREE

Cheap motels aplenty littered the edge of Greentown. Austin kept driving. He told the nav AI what he wanted and it piloted him there.

And while the low prefab buildings and neighborhoods slid by him, he tried not to think of anything—not Roan, not Grayson, and definitely not fucking JT. But you know how that works and he couldn't think of anything else.

So, yeah, what had he expected when he showed up two years out of nowhere? Had he really expected JT to drop his jeans right there and bend over ready for him?

Well, yeah. Kinda, he had.

What Austin'd expected: JT bent facedown over the Corvette's endless black hood; tight green ass thrust out over the fender for Austin to take; those heavy, swollen nuts ripe to blow; cock shoved straight down so Austin could see the skin-covered head of it leaking in streams. And a few centimeters above all of that: muscle-tight cheeks spread just enough to show JT's little puckered hole, just a bit pink, glossy with spit and twitching, daring Austin to open him up.

Well, it wasn't that crazy a thought, now was it? He'd brought him a damn car, after all.

The district was called Party Town for obvious reasons. He found a good parking space, street side, only a few blocks away from the bar, and that was fine because the walk would do him good.

Only a handful of humans or elves, but there were orcs everywhere, orcs going in, orcs coming out, crowds leaving restaurants, queuing for clubs, jaywalkers, street musicians, panhandlers. Bumper-to-bumper cars crawling along, taillights on and off, headlights flaring.

From the sidewalk, he fingered the car key (old-fashioned, not having any of the tech JT had) and popped the code on the security. Blue plasma arced over the Corvette and kept arcing like Borealis. Everyone slowed and gawked because it was just that pretty to watch. Just as pretty as Austin himself. Someone muttered, "Asshole," jealous as fuck. Austin ignored them all, hands in his pockets. He sauntered along, small smug grin, their envy an aphrodisiac. Ignored the hate.

The buildings here were low, two stories, and their windows were filled with holo-adverts and the air with a riot of overlapping noise. Somewhere a band played; he could feel the vibrating bass in the air. He wove through the crowd. Orc women (always punk haircuts, small-breasted, and built like world-class weight lifters) gave him a flick of their gaze, licked lips and tusks, and turned their heads back to their men slowly, letting them know they'd lost their attention to an elf.

In one window he saw Roan: big-ass hazy crown of her afro, points of her ears sticking through, broad white smile against the brown of her face, butterflies in her hair. He stumbled, shocked.

But it was only an advert, and it wasn't her anyway. It couldn't be her. Roan had been dead two years.

Shouldn't it have stopped after two years? Sure, right afterward, he'd thought he saw her everywhere, sure, right afterward. But now? Shouldn't this have stopped, not grown even more common, nearly every day; common enough he worried he was going insane?

JT had told him to let her go, but he couldn't do that. How could he? And how could JT have even asked Austin to let her go? She'd loved JT too. Loved him like a brother.

Austin saw half glimpses of her everywhere. Every dark-skinned woman with an afro became Roan. Every butterfly became the holo-decoration Roan had worn. He had gone insane, hadn't he? And he watched the advert loop and loop again. But it still wasn't Roan no matter how many times he watched it.

He knew the distraction he needed. There was the nightclub. Those orcs there, they'd clear his head. They'd appreciate him the way JT refused to.

The queue rippled when Austin's glamour brushed it. Noses flared, chests puffed, arms crossed, and muscles flexed. Every one of those men struck some pose to say they weren't to be fucked with and black eyes tracked him.

The bouncer at the door glittered with sex the way bouncers always did, like the job came with a glamour all its own. He wore a black T-shirt that said *STAFF* in what was meant to be block letters, except all the muscle underneath warped the letters out of shape. Austin ignored him, walked past, and that earned him a big green hand square in the middle of his chest.

"Felt your glamour a half a block away." STAFF had a broken brick of a nose, like a cartoon mafia thug. It was a good look for an orc, and Austin wondered if he'd paid for it or if he'd been one of the lucky ones. (JT's nose was as button as a Gerber baby's. Or so Austin would have thought if he'd let himself think about JT.) "You're trouble is what you are, and we don't need that here."

Austin cocked his head, puzzled, like that couldn't be true. "Ain't never been anyplace that didn't need a little trouble now and again."

STAFF leaned into Austin. He had good long tusks, the kind that made people joke about big hands and feet. He leaned in so close he almost grazed the skin of Austin's neck, so close Austin thought the orc was gonna kiss him or what passed for a kiss when you had tusks in the way. His brick-shaped mafia nostrils flared. They said the smell of fear was to an orc like seventy-percent chocolate or oysters or pomegranates was to everyone else. STAFF didn't smell anything but Ralph Lauren. "Not the crazy-fucker kind of trouble. The kind that don't know when they should run."

"I never run." Austin took the hand off his chest. That hand was thick and heavy. He missed the pressure of it when it was gone.

He walked on past. STAFF didn't stop him. Wasn't an orc in that queue who complained.

"If I have to come for you—" STAFF called behind him, but Austin didn't hear the rest of the promise.

It was an orc-only club in an orc ghetto-town lit for orc eyes, which meant hardly no lights at all, their eyes better than elves'. Strobes flickered, barely candlelight. Red and burnt orange washed the walls indirectly and made a hellish backdrop to the hulking silhouettes of a few hundred orcs, like this was the end of that remake of *Apocalypse Now* that had scared the shit out of everyone. The place smelled of orc-sweat and orc-sex so strongly the AC couldn't clear it. Most elves couldn't stand that smell. To Austin it was rich and sour like overturned earth, cured leather, leaf rot, and day-old gym shorts. It was incense, and this kind of place here was as close as Austin ever got to church.

Over the last two years, he'd come to places like this sometimes: orc-only bars where he'd stir up trouble. He'd pick a big one, one that looked like he could hurt Austin, and Austin would fuck him in the corner, or in the alley, or sometimes if he was drunk or high enough, he'd let them take him home and they'd make a whole night of it. (He only did that when he thought about JT. Like he wasn't doing now.)

Look at those orcs around him: shirtless, T-shirts tucked in belts, sweat-sheen-polished malachite muscle chests, biceps bound in straining bands, cocks and nuts bound up tight in jeans and leather just waiting for an excuse to bust. That one there: a full set of four tusks a good ten centimeters long flashed under strobe light. That one: ten kilos of spiked body piercings glittered. That one: arms big around as Austin's waist and crawling with bio-phosphorescent tattoos. And all of their eyes steamed red, hopped up on whatever party drug was in vogue this week. They'd eat Austin alive.

Well, that was the plan, wasn't it?

The bartender bought Austin's beer for him the way bartenders always did. Austin pressed through the crowd—back to back, chest to chest, cock to ass—and left a wake of unfocused lust behind him.

You wouldn't think orcs could dance, would you, but they danced like you imagined they did now that you've imagined it: frantic like a mosh pit, packed in so tight they were slick with one another's sweat. Austin circled around them, keeping distant because his glamour would turn that frenzy violent like a spark on gasoline. He kept to the cramped side spaces: places to talk if you didn't mind shouting, places to grope if you didn't mind an audience.

In one corner five younger orcs huddled tightly together, no gaps in the small circle they made of their bodies, intense and private, nothing but backs and bowed heads. They were jerking each other off, Austin knew. He stood at a table and watched them and wondered what they'd do with his glamour once they felt it.

A minute was all it took, and then their heads turned up and the five of them looked at one another more greedily than before, eyes all smoldering, and by some unspoken set of cues they picked one of the five—the littlest one, it always was—and shoved him down onto his knees amid them and the circle closed. Lucky little orc got to help out his friends. (The way JT should have done.) Austin smiled, proud of himself, like he was some rogue cupid who'd just made a match.

A heavy hand dropped onto his shoulder. "You're a public menace. It's time for you to go." It was STAFF. No surprise. Austin had known from the first touch, that hand on Austin's chest, that STAFF would be the one. Austin let STAFF steer him toward the door, knowing they'd never make it that far. He'd seen the orc's eyes. They'd gone orange like they reflected candlelight from somewhere, but there were no candles. (JT's would have gone orange with windblown sparks.)

And they didn't make it that far. They made it three meters. STAFF spun Austin to face him, backed Austin hard into a wall, and pinned him there with his big hands on Austin's shoulders. A lifetime of drawing a twenty-kilo bow and those hands still covered Austin's shoulders.

STAFF was a good-looking orc—strong nose and jaw and brow, everything about him strong—and the candle-fire in his eyes danced crazy, deep in Austin's glamour. He dragged his tusks across the skin of Austin's neck. He nipped and pulled at flesh until it snapped free of his teeth. There'd be marks tomorrow. (Good. Marks would make JT know what he'd missed.) "Maybe I should teach you when to run," STAFF said.

He took Austin's hand and guided it to his crotch and the hard ridge that strained beneath black denim. Tusks grazed Austin's neck again, up his throat into the soft underside of Austin's chin, so he had to tilt his head back or be hurt. (JT's tusks weren't so long.) The orc sucked at Austin's Adam's apple, warm tongue, hot breath smelling faintly of spearmint. (JT didn't chew gum.)

Austin threaded fingers through the orc's hair, longer like younger orcs wore theirs and sticking out every which way, orc bedhead. He ran his hand over the fabric covering STAFF's cock. (JT's jeans would have been damp, not dry.) STAFF was orc sized, nothing special. (JT was anything but.) Austin felt a hard loop at the tip of him. He undid STAFF's jeans and pulled the orc's dick free. He was cut and had a Prince Albert, so Austin tugged on it good and sharp like what it was meant for. STAFF bowed his head and pressed his forehead against Austin's chin. He sighed shakily.

"Why don't you get on your knees and suck me off," Austin said into the leaf-shaped, leaf-colored ear near his lips.

"No, we should go to my place."

"No, right here."

"I work here."

"So everyone will know you sucked off an elf. And everyone will wonder who he was."

Austin stroked the orc's tusks with his thumb because he knew they liked that. What did that feel like? Not like having your teeth rubbed, he didn't think. He ran his tongue along it. With his other thumb, he rubbed the bare head of the orc's cock and played with the piercing. (JT needed a piercing like that. Imagine what that'd look like hidden under all that foreskin. JT needed a half-dozen piercings like that.)

STAFF raised his fire-glazed eyes to Austin. "This is elf magic what you're doing to me, ain't it? This is your glamour messing with my head."

"Elf magic," Austin agreed.

"This ain't me."

"Nope. You got no choice," Austin agreed, happy to lie. A glamour amplified and elaborated; it didn't create. But some people needed an excuse to misbehave, and Austin liked being an excuse to misbehave.

So STAFF sank to his knees. Orcs around them made space. STAFF fumbled at Austin's belt and khakis. Austin unbuttoned his flowered shirt. He spread his legs as far as his fallen trousers would allow, clasped his hands behind his head, stretched, and leaned back against the wall. His shirt fell open. Hairless skin glared white. He grinned out at his admirers, perfect foxy V smile, as STAFF's lips closed around his cock. There. Warm and snug. This was how it was supposed to be.

Here's the Monet of it: Pale chest crisscrossed with paler scars, pale ears through mussed dark hair, a backdrop of darkness and fire. STAFF on his knees worshipping Austin's perfect cock—a block of dark green blotted out by dark clothes, *STAFF* in white letters so contrasting, they glowed. A gray clearing around the two of them. Then their audience: hulking shadows all square shoulders and sharp spikes against hell lights, paired dots of glowing red eyes. Six pairs. A dozen. Two dozen, as more turned to watch.

The thunder of music seemed to dim until everyone could hear the squelch of spit as STAFF sucked. Austin fed on their attention, need, lust, and envy, some of it for Austin, some for STAFF, some for both of them and couldn't decide if they'd rather be the elf or the orc.

"Is that Mikey?" one said.

"Shit, that's Mikey."

"Look at that."

"Who's the elf?"

Mikey, Austin thought. (It was JT's name they should have been saying.)

One hand drifted down, fingers ready for the sharpness of JT's close-cut sides, ready for the snapping bristle of the hair under his thumb, ready for it against his nuts, but found STAFF's shaggy head instead. So his hand went elsewhere, where it wouldn't remind him whose mouth he wasn't fucking.

He twisted at his own nipple, dug nails into it like they were orc teeth. (Too blunt, too soft, too shallow by far.) One of the orcs watching stepped forward to help. Mikey gave him a stay-the-fuck-back kind of look. The orc did. (JT would have growled. JT's eyes would have blazed. They'd have steamed. And every damn orc in that room would have stepped back, not just the one. JT would have made sure they all knew Austin's body was his and no one else's to touch.)

"Hey, Mikey, what's he taste like?"

"I hear elves taste like blueberries."

"I hear they taste like chicken." Orc laughter rumbled like too much bass.

Orc *dentata*: thirty-four teeth. Tusks between the lower canines and first bicuspid: three to ten centimeters in length. First bicuspid: one to three centimeters in length. Typically only the tusks protrude from the lips when the mouth is closed. Upper canines, sometimes called fangs, two centimeters in length, a distal gap to allow room for the tusks to grow through. There was no reason to believe that orcs had evolved. There had only been orcs for a generation and a half. But evolutionary biologists said those teeth were made to hold and tear big meat.

They scraped Austin's cock, jabbed at his thigh, and caught the skin of his balls, tiny jolts of pain to contrast against the soft, smooth warmth of STAFF's lips and tongue. Austin watched the orc suck. He was good. He knew how to use his tongue. One big hand held Austin's thigh for support. The other squeezed and pulled at his own pierced cock.

That cock would look good fucking JT. Maybe he had. This wasn't a JT kind of place—a JT kind of place had pool tables that people used for playing pool—but Greentown was small enough, so it could be that STAFF and JT had met somewhere.

He thumped STAFF on the temple to get his attention. "You ever fuck an orc named JT?"

STAFF shrugged and shook his head, and a tusk jabbed at Austin.

"You should," Austin said.

Yes, Mikey should. Mikey should slide that nice pierced cock into JT, seed him up good and slick, make JT ready so Austin could show them all how JT was really meant to be done. How you worked JT open. How you had to hold him down so he didn't thrash so much.

"You can crash on the couch."

No. That wasn't the thought to be having now, not while all these orcs watched Austin take their doorway hero in the mouth. He pulled STAFF's head down on him and the warmth of STAFF's mouth took everything Austin had.

"I'll get you some blankets."

So now JT had his own bed (not one rented or stolen, but a bed all his own), his own house, his own job, and his own kid protégé, and Austin wasn't welcome.

No, don't think about JT. Think about this orc here. This perfectly good orc right here where JT should have been.

His hands knotted in hair that was too long and held STAFF down on him so tusks dug in deep. *Well, fuck you, JT. Here's what you're fucking missing. It could have been you here on your knees with my cock deep down your throat. It could have been you these orcs were dreaming of. You they were hating jealous hate for. You they'd fight over when the fighting broke out (because fighting always broke out). Instead I'll fuck all these orcs here, one after another, and the lucky ones can tell their friends it tastes like goddamn strawberries.*

He pulled STAFF off him. Except STAFF wasn't gasping for air the way Austin had meant for him to. Austin had gone soft.

Goddamn JT. This was all his fault.

"What's wrong?" STAFF said, Austin's pretty dick in his hand, trying to knead it back to life.

"I stole him a fucking Corvette, for Christ's sake! What the hell else does he want?"

STAFF stopped stroking. "You stole a Corvette?"

Austin blinked. It was like someone had turned on the lights and all the magic of the place had been banished. Look at them all: dressed to intimidate, pierced to the nines. And not a one of those orcs looked as good as JT, not even Mikey the Doorman. And for all their pretending—all their piercings and patterned scars and tattoos and leather—not a one of them would be anywhere near as dangerous to fuck as JT was. And Mikey the Doorman on his knees with Austin's cock in his hand . . . he was probably just a nice down-home guy, and who wanted one of those? Those were a dime a baker's dozen. None of these orcs would feel as good as JT would. And one, or two, or a score of them, it wouldn't scratch the itch he had now that he'd seen JT again, now that the memories of him weren't two-years dimmed.

"You stole a Corvette?"

"Borrowed," Austin said. "Bought. I mean *bought*. I bought him a Corvette. Like rich people do. I'm rich."

"You know, if he's your boyfriend or something and you two need a third—"

"He ain't my goddamn boyfriend."

"What is he, then?"

Well, how the hell was Austin supposed to know what JT was? What kind of dumb-ass question was that? He pulled his dick out of the orc's hand and tucked it back in his khakis. "He's just a stupid orc."

STAFF looked confused and hurt. The candlelight in his eyes had died out, and Austin felt a bit guilty. "Look, it's not you; it's me." Austin winced because that sounded shitty. "You were right. I shouldn't have come here." He shook his head in frustration and started for the door.

The worked-up audience tried to stop him. Hands dropped on him, black nails dug into his shirt and grabbed at his belt.

"You ain't just walking off," one said.

"Gotta finish what you started," another said.

"You ain't leaving till we're done."

He gave them that look: the cold, dead one that came from years of lying and killing, being lied to and betrayed. He said, "Don't make this hard."

And every damn one of them let go and stepped back.

To Mikey, still on his knees, Austin pitched, "You want a good fuck, you find JT and tell him Austin sent you."

Out in the cool night, he gave one last glance to the window holo with its advert that wasn't Roan. Tomorrow, everything would start to make sense. It would all come together and the world would be made right, just like it had been back then. He slid into the car he had stolen for JT and headed out of town, out into the desert where he belonged and should have gone to begin with.

CHAPTER FOUR

ustin left the car behind and walked until he couldn't see the
lights of anything anymore. The desert ground was cold under
his bare feet: cold dirt and rock and sand spotted by spindly shrubs.
There was a light breeze hissing dust along, and overhead there
were so many stars, like it was a fairy-tale world. It felt good here.
There was none of the erratic tidal tug of people out here, and the
power in the earth flowed smooth and slow as continents sleeping on
molten beds.

The orcs had picked a good desert to build their strange little
paradise town. They'd been lucky the White Mountain Apache liked
them. Or maybe the tribe had just wanted their own army in case
what was left of the US government came knocking again.

Ahead was a flicker of golden light, and all the stress in Austin
drained away. The light streaked toward him. Austin, blind to
anything he was doing, awash with relief, walked faster toward it,
faster until he was running, until finally he slid, burning the knees
of his khakis thin, and the tiny ball of light leapt at him. He caught
it and held it to his chest and nuzzled it and said, "Hey there, boy,
hey Nebraska, hey," and nearly cried from the comfort the animal
gave him.

Nebraska was a fennec fox the size of a football. He was magical
and flickered with pale-golden light like starshine on a pond. Austin
cooed at his familiar and muttered all kinds of silly things, things he
would have denied had anyone overheard. "Yeah, I missed you too,"
he said, as if Nebraska had spoken to him. "He's just a big dumb orc.
You wouldn't like him anyway. Did you find me something? Come
on, show me what you found."

He set Nebraska down, and the fox darted off, and Austin pulled the power of the land up into him and set off after, fast as the fox, no trail behind him.

It was two months ago Austin had come down from Winchester Mountain with Nebraska in his arms. The summoning ritual had taken days, and Austin was dizzy from lack of food. He blinked three times before he was sure it was really Grandfather Henry who waited for him at the trailhead and not some hallucination. The old man was sitting at the base of a hemlock eating an apple, truck idling nearby, no explanation for how he'd known that now would be the hour Austin returned. Grandfather gave Austin's familiar a good look and nodded, satisfied.

That surprised Austin. "You can see him?"

"If you'd have done what I told you when you was younger, you two would have met long ago. A lot of suffering and confusion avoided."

"You can see him," Austin said again.

"It's my job to see magical things, innit?" He crunched into his apple and chewed messily. "Most will not see him. The ones who care for you, though, he might choose to reveal himself to them."

"That'll be a short list," Austin muttered.

He held the glittering fox up with both hands to the late-afternoon sun and looked into the star-filled eyes. Then Austin sighed, tipped his head to one side and grimaced like the creature had peed on him. "I don't mean to complain, but he's awfully small. He's really not like me at all. He should be a mountain lion or a tiger or a cheetah or something. Something with claws and teeth." The fox yawned and showed his tiny needle teeth. "Bigger teeth," Austin told him.

"It has your ears. What will you call it?"

"Nebraska."

"This is Washington."

"And I wasn't born in Texas, either. Neither of us belong here.

Nebraska." He held him to his chest. "It's just you and me, buddy. That's all there is."

Nebraska led him to a stone the size of a walnut. It was not a pretty stone. He nudged it with his paw. Austin picked it up. It had never been touched by anything living, and he could feel the power coalesced within it, enough to work magic by. "Good job. This will work great. Good job." He put the stone in the small bag he wore on his belt. Then the fox took off running again, and Austin kept up with the same unnatural speed and soft footfalls as before. This was part of the magic Nebraska had given Austin: the fox's speed and grace added to Austin's own.

Within an hour, Austin and his familiar had collected four more stones. Then he sat cross-legged in the desert, the fox curled in his lap. Austin looked out to the east and fell into that strange half sleep elves had, something closer to meditation than to human or orc sleep, though not quite that either.

And he couldn't put Roan aside, not even then. Not JT neither. But thoughts of those two stayed quiet like the people themselves standing at a respectful distance, and they didn't pull him off-center so long as he had Nebraska with him.

He watched the stars rise. He watched the planets crawl. He watched the moon pass overhead. He watched the long, slow nuclear bloom of dawn, and every moment of all those things was a quiet celebration.

When the sunlight broke the horizon and warmed him, Austin stirred. The world was all right. Austin was ready.

JT had already prepared the vehicle they'd take. It was a brightly painted pickup truck on oversized wheels. The cab was so high off the ground there were ladders on the side to get to the doors. Written along the side of the bed were the words *Country Orc* in cursive against a backdrop of airbrushed mesas and deserts, and horses with flowing manes and tails.

Austin's jaw dropped at the sight of it. "You can't be serious."

"This is my baby."

"This is an operation, not a carnival."

That earned Austin an icy glare. "This truck has got everything we need. Now get your things and let's go."

So much for starting off the day on better footing. From the non-trunk of the Corvette, Austin fetched a gym bag and a second, far larger, complicated-looking bag that carried his bow and arrows. He climbed the ladder to the cab and the door closed after him. The truck's cab had no controls whatsoever. It was undecorated and looked unfinished. The seat molded itself to Austin—same technology as the 'Vette used.

JT held out his hand to Austin. "Here."

"What?" But Austin held his hand out without waiting for an answer. JT dropped a rock in it. It was limestone and had a streak of green through it. Malachite probably.

"What's this?" Austin asked, but he could feel the magic in the rock.

"I couldn't sleep last night. So I went walking. I found that out in the desert. It was kind of pretty . . . Thought maybe . . ." He shrugged. "I don't know. I can never tell. Is it magic?"

Austin glanced from the rock to JT, but JT wasn't looking. Probably he was going through whatever startup systems he needed. "No," Austin lied, not knowing why he did. Maybe the idea of both of them out on their own in the desert hunting for rocks thinking of each other was too much to believe. Or maybe lying to JT was just a habit Austin couldn't break. "But it's a nice rock anyway." He slipped it into his bag with the five Nebraska had found for him. "Thanks."

And that was that: apologies and lies all told, they were back where they started. They pulled out of the compound, San Francisco bound.

CHAPTER FIVE

They argued over music because JT refused to play anything written this century. They argued what direction to take into town because Austin thought it was more dramatic to come to the rescue via the Golden Gate rather than the Bay Bridge. Comfortable arguments, an easy rhythm to fall into.

They came in by the Bay Bridge listening to nothing. JT activated the truck's transponder and the Bay Area Traffic Net added the vehicle to the millions it managed. JT had old override codes tied to emergency response vehicles and VIPs, but they would splash the system when activated and someone would be bound to notice the waves. Best hold them until needed. "I haven't kept this software up-to-date," he said. "I really hope those codes still work."

Austin shrugged. "You'll figure something out. Always do." Austin stared out the window and JT did also, just as much a passenger as Austin now that BATN had taken over the truck. The Embarcadero glowed multihued through a thin fog, and the half-lit office buildings of downtown were a patchwork of blue-green blocks and streaks against black. Near the north edge of downtown, the Sorcerer's Tower, five hundred meters high, twice the height of the graceless pyramid it had replaced, shimmered like water. Its rainbow of arcane sigils floated up its sides, broke away, and drifted like clouds written over the city. Some people said a dragon lived in its pinnacle. JT thought that was bullshit. Most of the time.

The city was beautiful.

JT's desert was more beautiful still. And Dante and Duke and the others, they were all there. All there was here was Buzz. And the dead.

"Where you been living?" JT asked, afraid to ask because so far they'd skirted around things like that.

"Wherever I'm sleeping."

"The City?" The way Austin had been after Roan's death, it was easy to imagine him lingering in SF, obsessed like a ghost. That had been the path Austin had been heading down, hadn't it?

"Sometimes," Austin said, obviously as unwilling to have this conversation as JT was.

Pylons and cabling slid by. They were nearing the end of the bridge and BATN was requesting a destination update.

"So where is Buzz holed up? How do we find him?"

"He said he'd put up markers. City Netspace, I suppose."

"And we're just supposed to drive the streets looking for Netspace markers? We might never find him."

City Netspace was a virtual reality that overlaid the city's real space. Anyone with VR glasses or networking implants could access it. In its early days, it had carried tourism and historical information, making the city a museum of itself, including superimposed archival images dating back to the eighteen hundreds. All that information was still there, hyperlinked to academic papers and documentary footage. But after endless vandalism by hackers and virtual artists, the city administrators had thrown up their hands and opened the network to the public. The result had been a palimpsest of virtual graffiti that had begun the Fog City Renaissance back in the fifties. It was a part-genius, mostly-useless chaotic mess of graphics and animation wrapped ghostly over real-world space, perfect for artists, activists, and criminals.

JT accessed the Netspace and winced as the city went lurid with gang tags, one hundred meter adverts for every damn thing and then some, pornography, and Escherian trompe l'oeil architecture. He looked back at the Bay to see if Godzilla was still there, and he was, splashing around. Godzilla had always been there and always would be. No hacker ever messed with Godzilla. And if JT could have seen the ocean from here, no doubt there'd still be the water-walking Gundam battalion endlessly invading Pacifica.

He searched for a 3djinn tag—an asterisk made from three crossed scimitars—and found nothing.

"There," Austin said, but Austin couldn't even see into Netspace, so how he knew— "There," Austin said again and pointed. The mark wasn't in Netspace at all, and it wasn't a 3djinn tag.

There was a monarch butterfly on the windshield, except monarchs were extinct. *Roan*, he thought. He said her name aloud before he could stop himself, and heartbeats of silence passed. Then he said, "That's not real. That's magic. Buzz has a wizard?"

Austin shrugged. The butterfly fluttered away.

They followed it through the Financial District, skating right past the Tower ("You think a dragon really lives up there?" "How should I fucking know?") and into North Beach, where the butterfly's route became erratic.

"I can't tell BATN to follow a butterfly."

"Park. We'll follow on foot."

"You sure?"

Austin shrugged.

JT put in the request to park and ten minutes later they were on the top level of a garage on Broadway. He blackened the windows, and Austin suited up, tying himself up in velcro straps and nylon string, bow, arrows, knives, and magic stones all where he wanted them, hands moving like getting dressed was some stage magician's trick.

"Jesus, JT, do I have to tell you? Check your pistol."

"What do I need a pistol for?"

"To kill things before they kill you?"

"There's a pistol under the seat." JT had never needed to use it. If something came after him that could punch through this truck, he'd need more than a pistol to stop it.

"Under the seat won't do you any good when you're out there with me."

"Out there with you?" JT laughed, then stopped abruptly. "Are you fucking serious?"

"What the hell did you think I got you for?"

"Maybe you don't remember, Austin, but I'm a glorified getaway driver. That and the bots—that's all I do. Grayson had your back, not me."

"Grayson's dead. You aren't. And you're coming with me."

"We don't know where that bug's going to take us. We get over the hill, I'll lose the truck signal and we lose the drones."

"Figure it out."

"I don't know the first thing about feet-on-the-ground work."

"Time to learn." Austin went for the door handle, but there wasn't one. "Door, please?"

JT took the pistol from under the seat and slaved it. He took two clips from the glove box and stuffed them in the pocket of his jeans.

Jeans. Look at Austin in his military ninja costume looking like some anime hero. Now look at JT in his blue jeans and sleeveless flannel looking like he didn't know what. *All I ever wanted to do was fly planes. Look at me now.*

JT popped the doors and climbed down out into the cool night air of San Francisco, as ready as he'd ever be, which was hardly at all.

Once Telegraph Hill had been high-class. Not anymore. The alley here was tight and filled with sodden litter and rubbish bins. Over the door, an old incandescent bulb sparked like it was about to explode. Beside the door was an old vid panel. The camera on it glowed red like the eye of a pissed-off orc to show it was on. On top of the panel an extinct monarch butterfly fanned its wings.

JT had dropped one land-bound bot as a repeater to strengthen the signal between himself and the truck. Four airborne drones—not much more than cameras and assault guns on toy helicopters—circled the rooftops and scanned alleys. A second land-bound bot stood beside JT, a sturdy four-legged spider, waist high. People always thought controlling drones was like watching a battery of monitors. It wasn't like that at all. Drones were like removable hands and eyes, and it had taken years of training, a hundred thousand dollars of software, and a dangerous amount of black market neuropsychoactive drugs to make JT's brain into something that could process multi-ocular vision for sustained periods of time without suffering a breakdown. With six drones and the truck slaved to him, JT felt immense, spread out, cloud-like, fog-like, and that runty green body was only the smallest part of what he was.

He watched the streets and rooftops and alleys all at once. He saw nothing out of the ordinary, and that made him edgy because it seemed far more likely that seeing nothing meant he'd missed something, not that there was nothing to see.

The door clicked open. Stairs, so JT left the bot behind. The butterfly led them up two flights, then down a corridor, past several doors, to the door at the end.

The butterfly vanished as the door opened. Beyond was a sorcerer's apartment. He could tell from all the weird shit. There were enough lava lamps to light a disco, though what bubbled in them wasn't wax, and the blobs in the one on the coffee table looked remarkably like an orc and an elf standing in a doorframe. The walls were covered in so many hand-painted arcane symbols they overlapped one another. There were even symbols on the ceiling. The paint had been slopped on too thick or too quick and had run in places like the walls were bleeding. A mobile made from the skeletons of small animals hung in the corner of the room. Its tiers spun lazily as the skeletons ran or flew or crawled on the air. And there wasn't a bit of digital technology anywhere; even the clock was pendulum-powered.

The wizard sat cross-legged in the air next to his oracular lava lamp. He wore pajama pants and a red plush bathrobe, open to show his scrawny chest. He had long straight black hair and that mix of features and skin tone you got when you threw five different ancestries into the West Coast blender. His eyes were silver, actual silver orbs engraved with writing. Blue-violet plasma arced from one hand to the other, a spell he was just waiting for an excuse to throw at them.

And that was okay, because Austin had an arrow nocked, and one of JT's drones aimed its cannon though a window at the wizard's back.

Then there was Buzz. Buzz was an Irish human. Not black-haired Irish like Austin, but the other kind. He was shorter than JT, had curly ruddy-brown hair that would have shown copper in the sun, and big brown eyes. They were red-rimmed and bruised like he hadn't slept in days. He was a bit on the stocky side; it showed in his freckled cheeks. He was just short of painfully cute.

JT couldn't help but smile. He'd made the right choice by coming here, and he and Buzz—

"What'd you bring that animal here for?" Buzz said to Austin.

"Animal? What—"

All the warm happy glow died out of JT. "Hi, Buzz," he said with a tone that meant *Fuck you.*

"Victor," Buzz said to the wizard. "That orc comes after me, you can zap him."

Austin shifted his aim from the floor to the wizard. "No! No, Victor, whoever the hell you are, you cannot zap the orc."

JT shrugged helplessly. "Buzz, come on . . ." He'd barely even moved, but Buzz honestly flinched like JT was on the attack, and shouted, "Keep away from me, you cannibal!"

The plasma in Victor the Wizard's hand snapped in warning.

That worked JT's nerves. "It's not cannibalism if you ain't the same species, Buzz. It's just dinner."

Five meters away, and JT felt that plasma go hotter.

"Everyone stop it!" Austin put up his hands, arrow in one, bow in the other. "Everyone put your weapons down!" Austin slowly put his bow and arrow down on the battered parquet floor. "You, Victor, get rid of that whatever it is you're doing there with that light. Get rid of it!" The plasma dimmed to violet, but didn't go out. "Good enough. Excuse us. JT, can I have a word with you?" Austin didn't wait for an answer. He hauled JT into the hall. "What the hell is going on?"

"I might have bit him."

"You 'might have bit him'?"

JT shrugged. "I might have been worked up. You get an orc worked up, you know things might happen."

"Worked up? Oh my God, you slept with him?"

Well, no, they hadn't quite gotten that far, but JT didn't like the judgmental tone. "And what's wrong with that?"

"It's Buzz, that's what's wrong with that."

"He's a nice guy."

"He's Buzz."

JT's startup business had required credit, and credit required an official history, something neither JT nor Austin had ever had. They'd both been born off the grid and had stayed off the grid, using stolen IDs when they needed temporary legitimacy. So when JT decided to leave his old life and build a new one, Buzz had been the natural choice to turn the fictional Jason Taylor into a real person, a person who could take out loans, sign legal papers, and pay taxes. Buzz was an artist. It had taken him six weeks to plant the evidence of a life lived: not just birth records and a SIN, but traffic tickets, a college degree, a master's thesis, tax forms, annual employee reviews, even a student loan default. And when all those databases had been hacked and signatures forged and it was done, the two of them had sat on Buzz's old beat-up couch and watched a holo of JT's new record—Jason Taylor—turn lazily in the air, and celebrated.

Out of nowhere, Buzz had stolen a nervous peck of a kiss, and JT had turned to him high as a kite and so damn grateful, and Buzz was so damn cute, all redheaded Irish, and who'd say no to that? Not anyone sensible. Seconds later, shirts were off, JT had Buzz pinned beneath him, and Buzz's mouth had tasted like pot, and his sweet eager fear of JT had been a cologne that sent JT higher than any weed.

"I didn't sleep with him, okay? But I would have. If I hadn't bit him first. And he hadn't kicked me out. It really didn't bleed all that bad."

"That's why you said yes to this job. You got a thing for Buzz."

"I don't have a thing. We have some history. I wasn't gonna let him get killed."

"*History*," Austin said and let the word hang there between them like it had some significance. "I wish I'd known that before. I wouldn't have gone through all the trouble of getting that car. Let's get this over with so you can get back to that nice, quiet, real life of yours." He turned and went back into the apartment, leaving JT alone in a hallway that had just gone very, very chilly.

"JT Jameson," Victor the Wizard said, using a name JT hadn't gone by in years, with a greasy awe that JT didn't trust one bit, "and Austin Shea. Legends in the flesh."

"And who the hell are you?" Austin asked.

"Victor the Wizard, Transmuter and Bearer of the Silver Eyes of Horus."

Austin rolled his eyes. "Right. Buzz, what's he here for? We didn't talk about bringing in a wizzy on the job."

"I prefer the full term 'wizard.'"

They were all sitting around the coffee table as if they were best friends planning a night out, except that Victor was still floating and watching his magical lava lamp, and Buzz was bouncing one leg like he was going to vibrate it off. The room was still chilly, and JT rubbed his arms.

"I did it, Austin." Buzz smiled so broad and proud, it made one dimple show.

"I know you brought him in, Buzz. I want to know why."

The windows weren't open. It was Austin's glamour making JT shiver. He leaned toward the elf. "Why are you pissed at me? What did I do?"

"I ain't pissed at you, JT."

Buzz leapt up from his chair and drew a crystal data block from his shirt pocket with a flourish. It went iridescent with refracted lava light. "No, I mean, I *did* it. I stole the Blue Unicorn just like you said." He bounced in place like he'd just made the winning goal, one hand in the air waiting for the onslaught of high fives.

Everyone stared at him and didn't say anything. No one jumped up to high-five him. Buzz's excitement ebbed, and he stopped bouncing. He scowled at them all. "I know that wasn't the plan. It's called improvisation. Thinking on your feet? Adaptability? It's considered a strength." And his hand went up again, giving everyone a second chance at high fives.

They all leapt up shouting, none of it congratulations. Austin shouted curses. JT shouted at Austin, "You told Buzz to steal a data block from the Triad?"

"I told him to wait until you and I got here."

"You told me you were hiding from a gang, not a triad," Victor said to Buzz.

"You told me this was a *rescue* operation," JT said to Austin.

"A triad is a gang."

"This is a rescue operation."

"You were not candid with me, Buzz," Victor said.

"You lied to me, Austin," JT said.

"I may have meant to, but as it turns out, I didn't." Austin rounded on Buzz. "I told you to wait!"

"You would have done the same thing!" Buzz said.

"You're not me. You could have blown the whole fucking thing!"

"I was just—"

"You've put me at risk, Buzz!" Victor said.

"I didn't mean—"

"Leave him alone!" JT bellowed and stepped in front of Buzz. "Both of you leave him alone!" The room was too small for an orc to be bellowing. It rattled the mobile with its little skeletons and they ran/flew/crawled faster until they tangled themselves in a mess. JT's heart pounded like a war drum. He was running dangerously hot, so huffed a couple of deep breaths to calm himself down, but that just showed how much muscle there was to him, like a bull snorting in the ring. Even Austin shut up and took a step back. The anxious tension in the room was too much, too distracting, and he couldn't hold on to his drones like this.

It was Austin's glamour, Austin's glamour fanning JT's orc blood into a wildfire. "Your glamour, Austin. Move farther away." Austin did and the hot edge of JT cooled like a newly forged blade hitting oil. Deeper breaths. Deeper. "We need to be on the road. We need to be on the road now."

He went to the window.

"Where are you going?" Austin said.

"Fire escape. Roof. I'm going to call the truck and I'll get a better signal up there." *And I'll be farther away from all of you.*

JT didn't have to be anywhere near his truck to drive it as long as he had a good signal, and with the Traffic Net there was even less to do: power up the truck, give BATN a destination, wait. Five minutes was the ETA BATN gave, which seemed like a goddamn long time, considering, but JT was still unwilling to try the emergency responder codes. They'd just have to wait.

And he was going to wait up here, alone, watching the fog, everything quiet. Sweet goddess, he loved the quiet. It was always surprising how quiet the City got at night with the fog. Like the desert. Or like the desert had been until Austin showed up with his damn car and his glamour and his lies.

JT heard climbing on the ladder and said, "Austin, I really don't want to talk to you right—" Before he flipped a camera there and saw it was Buzz. "Oh. You probably shouldn't be out here."

Buzz hesitated, then came up the rest of the way anyway. Buzz leaned against the parapet that surrounded the roof, a safe meter between him and JT, and they watched the streets fill up with fog. He said, "Thanks for that down there."

"You shouldn't have listened to Austin."

"It wasn't his idea. It was mine."

"No, it wasn't. It was Austin's. He's good at making you think his ideas are yours."

"No, it really was mine."

JT sighed and shook his head. "You're welcome."

Even the rooftop wasn't far enough away. JT still felt the tug of him. He felt Austin the way a planet felt the sun, that same inescapable running-away and falling-in that only ended when you burned up.

"And look, I shouldn't have said . . . about the whole cannibal thing . . ." Buzz winced. "Austin didn't tell me he was bringing you in, so you surprised me, was all. I suppose I should have figured it, but I guess I didn't think you'd come after I . . ." He shook his head and looked uncomfortable, and JT kind of liked that and wasn't about to interrupt him. "I'm not used to orcs—I mean look at you. You're huge and you've got tusks and your eyes glow red and—"

"I get it, I'm scary." He was still angry and didn't want to be, and he blamed that on Austin's glamour too.

Buzz looked away, guiltily, down into the fog. "I don't want to be that guy anymore. I'm tired of working in the background. I'm tired of being safe. I want to be the one people talk about."

This was Austin talking, not Buzz. This was how Austin did it. Always the lies. Always his glamour messing with everyone's head until no one knew what they really felt about anything. Once was a time JT actually thought he'd been in love with him, crazy as it sounded. Well, fuck Austin. Fuck him. JT wasn't gonna let Austin mess with him anymore.

"Kiss me," JT said.

"What? Are you sure? This isn't a good time, is it?"

They were alone—all clear for six blocks. They had four more minutes to kill, and Buzz needed to get his damn priorities straight. "You want to prove you're not afraid, then kiss me. Right now."

"Okay. Yeah." Buzz laid his left hand against JT's chest, slowly, like he was petting a dangerous dog, and cussed at how rock-hard the muscle there was. He cocked his head up, JT ten centimeters taller than him. JT closed his eyes and didn't move, not wanting to scare him.

A drone turned and watched as Buzz kissed him, featherlight, as sweet as the kiss Buzz had stolen eighteen months before.

Buzz leaned in closer, right hand on JT's biceps, grip barely covering the one muscle, and kissed JT again, firmer, longer. Buzz's lips parted. His hands slid down JT, chest to waist, biceps to forearm, forearm to JT's hand, fingers intertwining. There was something about handholding more than the kiss: the honesty of it, the simplicity of it (things Austin could never give). And JT couldn't keep still anymore. His arms went around Buzz, and Buzz stiffened, afraid, then relaxed and let it happen.

Last two years, JT had stuck mostly to orcs, and it was so nice to hold a body smaller than his, not hyper-muscled or elven perfect. For once JT didn't have to be special. He was just an everyday orc holding an everyday guy that he liked to hold—a quiet guy, a nice guy, a guy like the fog or the desert.

So JT held him tighter. He nuzzled his tusks against Buzz's freckled cheek, down his neck to his shoulder, careful not to hurt him, not even a scratch. But Buzz's fear came anyway, and it went straight to JT's head. He went a bit dizzy. His cock thickened, and JT could feel his pulse down in his balls. Through a drone's eyes, he could see his own eyes narrow, hungry, and fleck with red. This was how it had all gone pear-shaped last time.

He pushed Buzz away, one oversized hand against Buzz's cheek.

"No," Buzz said. Buzz's eyes were dilated wide and dark. He turned his head so JT's black-nailed thumb lay across his lips, then he sucked the thumb into his warm, soft mouth, and JT laughed, it felt so good. Buzz smiled at him, goofy looking with an orc's thumb stuck in his mouth.

JT let his other hand slide down to Buzz's crotch. Good and hard, same as JT. "What color's your hair down there?"

Buzz grimaced. "Orange."

JT grinned, all tusks and fangs. "We're gonna look like an Irish flag when you fuck me." He pulled Buzz in and held him around the waist. Their cocks rubbed through denim, and JT felt the cool damp of pre-come in his shorts.

The Electric Dragon Triad opened fire from a kilometer away.

CHAPTER SIX

Austin watched JT climb out onto the fire escape and up.
"Your glamour interacts poorly with the orc's blood," Victor the Wizard said.

"My glamour interacts just fine, same as the rest of me," Austin said with a sharp glance at Buzz.

Buzz? Seriously? What did Buzz have that Austin didn't? Out of shape, pasty, naive, spineless. Okay, he was Irish, so that counted for something (though it was hard to imagine Austin and Buzz sharing the same ancestry no matter how far back you went). And, okay, so Buzz had stolen the Blue Unicorn, and that took some balls (but it was still stupid as shit). And "history"? Seriously, Buzz and JT had "history"? Well what about Austin and JT? They had history. A lot more fucking history than some kiss that went bad. Austin and JT, they had whole years that went bad.

"You shouldn't have lied to him," Buzz said.

"He would never have come if I hadn't lied."

"The Triad will destroy my home," Victor the Wizard said. "I want a cut."

Buzz said, "There isn't—"

"One-quarter, even split," Austin said. As much as he didn't like wizards, they could use one.

"Austin, we aren't—" Buzz complained.

Add to Buzz's list of shortcomings: he was too honest by half. Austin would break the news to Victor that they weren't getting paid after the dust settled. "Shut up, Buzz. One-quarter, Vic. And you're coming with us."

"Agreed."

"I can't believe you." Buzz went to the window.

"Where are you going?" Austin said.

"To find JT."

"If you're going up there, give me that data block."

"No. I stole it. I'm holding on to it." And he climbed out onto the fire escape.

Austin huffed and plopped down into an overstuffed chair. He pulled out one of his magic-filled stones without looking. It was the one JT had given him. He frowned and chose another. He drew it along arrow heads, transferring their magic, and enchanted sparks flew.

Austin and Victor sat quietly, attention on the lava lamp between them. Its red globs bubbled the same way a lava lamp normally did, except occasionally the bubbles almost looked like something the way clouds almost looked like something. When that happened, Victor would wave his hand and the globs would flow backward, then forward again. Finally he would drop his hand and the lamp would go back to its normal abnormality.

Victor said, "Your glamour is remarkably strong."

"It ain't easy being me." What were they doing up there on the roof?

"Volatile as orcs are, it's a wonder JT can tolerate it. Even I can feel it."

"Yeah, and what's it feel like?" He could ask Victor to look in on them, but that might give the wizard the wrong impression. Austin didn't get jealous. Getting jealous meant you felt inadequate.

"It feels old."

"I'm twenty-six." Jealousy meant you felt second-best.

"Like a secret."

"That's me: Austin Shea, elf of mystery." Jealousy meant you felt flawed.

"Like if I only looked closer, I would learn something no one else knew," Victor the Wizard said softly.

So it couldn't be jealousy. Maybe Nebraska could take a quick peek? A mostly invisible familiar was as discreet as it got.

"If you let me study you, Austin—"

Austin's clothes snapped, he moved so fast. Victor blinked his strange silver eyes at the arrow against his throat. Austin whispered into the wizard's ear, "No one will ever study JT or me again. Ever. Do you understand?" Austin was probably overreacting, but he wanted to make sure his point wasn't lost. He didn't like wizards. He especially didn't like wizards who had a disproportionate interest in the strength of his glamour.

Victor nodded carefully toward the lava lamp. "It's starting." The not-wax had formed itself into a stream of objects like parading ants. It took Austin a moment to process the scene: not ants, bullets. Austin let Victor go, all offenses forgotten, and Victor's eyes went argent with power.

The spray of 20-mm bullets left the dual-rotored Kydoimos 647 Nightshrike gunship at 550 meters per second. Given loss of velocity due to drag, three seconds to impact. Target: two men standing in close proximity on a rooftop. The men would hear the shockwave of the supersonic bullets—a loud crackle—a moment before they died. Not enough warning for anything.

Except that Drone Four detected the multiple shockwaves at 100 meters out and transmitted the sound to JT via narrow microwave. JT recognized the sound immediately, about 95 nanoseconds, which gave him almost a half second to react.

And except that Victor the Wizard's oracular lava lamp was keyed to find threats, not sounds, and had a range determined mostly by aetheric confluences. In fact, it didn't understand distance any more than it understood past or future. Inexactness all around. So Victor had no idea how long he had to deliberate over the transmutation of a cloud of 100 gram bullets into something less deadly (though with equivalent mass and still traveling at around 300 meters per second). So he did the first thing that came to mind.

"Duck," JT said and tackled Buzz down to the solar-paper roof. With nothing to hide behind but scrawny ventilation tubes, a small profile was the only defense they had.

JT sent all four airborne drones toward the Triad gunship, and braced himself for the impact. He buried his face into Buzz's hair. If you're about to die, priorities.

Thuds all around him, strangely dull for bullets. Cold wet sprayed over him. Cold trickled down his cheek. "What the hell?" he said and rose up and looked. He rose too far up, and a loose-packed snowball the size of a softball hit him in the shoulder and exploded. It hit hard as a hammer; there'd be a bruise. More snowballs came in—*bam bam bam bam bam*—a wide spray of them that left white streaks on the rooftop and snow bursts on the low walls.

"That's Victor," Buzz said.

"Let's go!" JT hauled him standing. They scrambled, crouching low through the storm of snow, to the fire escape. He checked all his eyes: the fire escape and alley were clear. Drone Two in the apartment building foyer saw nothing, all clear. Drone One was still on repeater duty.

Drones Three through Six saw the gunship. The gunship saw them and switched targets.

Down the ladder: Buzz first, JT hot after. *Clang*, as they hit the landing.

The truck was still one minute out. JT sent the emergency responder code to take it off the Traffic Net. What the hell was the Triad thinking, pulling out firepower like that? Gunfire over the city would trigger a citywide traffic lockdown. What the hell had Buzz stolen?

As JT ducked through the window back into Victor's apartment, he caught shadows across the street flitting up and down walls and through fog. He thought they were police fliers, but there was no way to know; all his eyes were one K away engaging the gunship.

Buzz followed him into Victor's weird, lava-lit living room.

BATN rejected his first ER code, his second, his third. They were all too old, obsolete. BATN locked down JT's truck just like he'd expected. They weren't going anywhere.

"We're trapped," he told everyone.

"You okay?" Austin asked them.

"Yes." And JT fell into his old coordinator's role, second nature. "Nightshrike a kilometer southeast, Drones Three through Six engaged, repositioning Drone One"—along streets gone deathly quiet—"Drone Two, front door, all clear, blind on the rooftop and alley. No, there's something on the street."

It hadn't been the SFPD he'd seen. It had been 49ers, triad foot soldiers, called that for the numerological significance, not for the football team. They were running windowsill to windowsill, wall-crawling effortlessly, dressed in black, with runeblades flashing red and QCW-10 submachine guns shoulder-slung.

"49ers. Opening fire." And they heard the rattle of Drone Two's guns from below. Tenants awoke in neighboring buildings. JT heard their cries of panic through electronic ears.

"Austin, cover the fire escape window. Buzz, I need emergency responder codes for BATN. Are you linked up?"

"On it," Buzz said, and though he looked pale and shaken as any sane person would, he sat cross-legged on the floor and then slumped, looking for all the world like he'd fainted.

And seeing Buzz go into a hacker's trance the way Roan used to do, JT almost changed his mind. Buzz was a forger—he didn't belong in a gunfight. On the job that had gone bad, Roan had been sitting right next to JT in the van, not a meter away, looking just like Buzz did now, like any hacker did when they went deep in. And five minutes later, when all hell broke loose, blue fire had shot out the top of her head and she was dead. JT almost said, *Stop, Buzz. Never mind. We'll find some other way.*

JT didn't say it. Worse, he froze completely.

Things happened around him that didn't register the way they should. There was Austin at the window with his bow and a handful of arrows, firing out into the alleyway—at what, JT didn't know—broadheads sparking through the air as he whispered old elvish magic over them. There was Victor over a lava lamp working some kind of spell, his eyes glowing argent, and an immense, endless crash as the fire escape fell away from the building.

"Still coming!" Austin yelled.

But what just had happened JT couldn't form, all of it dreamlike and slow, none of it sensical except . . . Buzz was sitting there the way Roan used to do, the way she'd done just before she died.

Data flooded through JT's head, visions of things he shouldn't have been able to see: four different views of a bi-rotor helicopter, air filled with tracers and SFPD fliers ascending (real ones this time). He saw a street littered with wounded. Someone with a scarred riot shield threw a grenade toward him (toward Drone Two).

He saw the suppressor of a QCW-10 sneak around a fire-escape window. Austin didn't see it.

The grenade popped. Whiteout, then blackout, and Drone Two was lost.

An encrypted code appeared in JT's head. Buzz opened his eyes and smiled. "Done!"

A black-gloved finger pressed the trigger of a QCW-10.

"Down!" Austin shouted and dove. Victor tried his snowball thing again, but his concentration broke and he had to dive too. And there was Buzz just sitting there. Buzz. The one thing that made sense to JT: Buzz.

The gun sprayed bullets wide and blind, and JT threw himself through all of it toward Buzz. *Thup-thup-thup*, shots quieter than the impacts, and bullet-shattered shelving, plaster, and cushion stuffing erupted everywhere. JT hit Buzz hard ("What the fuck, JT!") and both of them sprawled behind a divan. The bullets kept on, and JT held him still while Buzz panicked and tried to get away. Lava lamps burst, water and glass. The lamps' captured air spirits broke free and zipped around, smashing everything the bullets hadn't before returning to some other world.

The bullets stopped, clip emptied. Three 49ers slipped in through the window, submachine guns and swords up, but Austin was up too, long knives out, and the first 49er didn't even touch the floor before Austin had cut her throat. The second wheeled on Austin. Austin parried his with his knife and flame spat as the two blades slid along each other. Fire drizzled over the floor. The third raised her gun, but at a word from Victor, it became a viper and bit her three times. She fell screaming and thrashing, and the viper clattered to the floor, a gun again.

JT transmitted the code Buzz had stolen and freed his truck from lockdown. He pulled drones Three through Six away from the

Nightshrike and police fliers. Let them battle it out—he needed his drones here.

Austin against the last 49er: parry, parry-riposte, feint with his left, and through the 49er's heart with his right. The 49er slid to the floor. Austin flourished his killing blade and blood spattered the eyes of soldier number four, already through the window. The foot soldier fired blind and hit nothing that hadn't already been ruined, then Austin killed him too. The window became a wall.

"Why didn't you do that before?" Austin said to Victor.

Victor the Wizard shrugged. "Didn't think of it."

Victor's eyes were tarnished dull and nowhere as bright as they'd been before. JT guessed they worked like Austin's rocks and their wizard was almost tapped out of mojo.

"Are you going to tackle me every time someone shoots at me?" Buzz squirmed to get out from underneath him. JT liked the feeling of Buzz squirming under him.

"Until you learn to duck, yes." JT stung all over, from bullet wounds or debris, he didn't know. But Buzz was safe, Buzz was safe. He gave Buzz his hand and helped him up.

Austin laid a hand on JT's shoulder. "Hey, you okay?" From the quiet with which he said it, the deep concern of his face, the weight of his hand, and the warmth of his glamour closing around JT like a childhood blanket, JT knew Austin didn't mean diving through a hail of bullets. Even in the middle of his own fight, Austin had noticed JT had lost it. And for a moment JT was trapped in Austin's soft, golden-flurried eyes. Almost, JT's heart felt ready to burst. He let go of Buzz's hand because just then Buzz couldn't ever be enough. For one heartbeat, JT stood confused, rawly in love, the two years apart from Austin a bad dream.

JT shook himself from his confusion and gently shrugged Austin's hand from him, now not the time, and said, all business, "Drone Two's down, and they've probably taken the stairwell. The Nightshrike's pulled back. It was a distraction to get me to send the drones off so a ground attack would work, and it did. I've called them back. Police fliers are tied up with the Nightshrike, but they'll be coming soon enough. Truck is on its way. We need a way down to the street."

"Okay then," Austin said as if that was an answer to his question. "Vic?"

"Vic-*tor*. Victor the Wizard. Victor the Transmuter."

From the stairwell, gunshots punched holes through the door.

Victor the Wizard waved at the floor. It disappeared, and they all fell down.

JT and Buzz half fell, half clambered down the hole Victor had made. Victor descended floating, and Austin jumped like the three-meter drop was nothing but a step. On the way, they glimpsed someone else's living room, hands over faces stifling their terror in the corner. Then Victor did it again, then again, and they ended up in a car-less garage, street level. They scattered away from the holes above them.

Above, someone shouted, "*Tóuxiáng*! *Tóuxiáng*!" Surrender. Like it wasn't a few minutes too late for that. Then the triad soldiers found the hole in the floor and one of them shot a burst down it into the garage floor. Everyone flinched and covered their heads.

"Out the door, right, down the hill. Austin, cover," JT said, and they all nodded. JT had a view from Drone One clacking its way up the hill: there were a half-dozen 49ers outside. They had QCW-10s like the ones before, suppressors on, all aimed at the front door of the apartment building. And it sounded like the 49ers upstairs were coming back down.

Time to go. JT popped the lid on Drone One, prioritized targets, checked his truck (ETA thirty seconds), checked his airborne drones (ETA twenty), and opened fire on the soldiers outside. A few flailed and hit the ground, dead or wounded; the rest scattered, took cover, and returned fire.

JT hauled the garage door open and everyone ran out onto the street and to the right just like he'd told them to.

Behind them, four men from the apartment stairwell charged out the front door. JT heard the hiss of Austin's magic arrows. He glanced back to watch (because it was impossible not to). Austin was running backward. He vaulted from a fire hydrant like it was a spring, hit the wall of a building, ran a few steps along it, then back-flipped to the ground. The 49er's bullets tracked him all the way, striking a moment behind him, exploding wood, concrete, and asphalt. He returned fire: five arrows as he leapt and tumbled. Each arrow streamed fire behind it and dropped a 49er. One arrow dropped two. The fires stayed where they were, twisting and snapping like pennons in a gale, and made a loose net the 49ers couldn't cross.

Sweet fucking goddess, where had Austin learned that? JT stumbled and bowled into Buzz and Victor both—they'd stopped running—and they all nearly went down in a heap. JT started to cuss them, then saw why they'd stopped.

In front of them stood a man in Ming dynasty gold, red, and black robes, embroidered at the hems with white chrysanthemums. He wore a jade mask, jade rings on all his fingers, and a necklace of tiny jade skulls. In his hand he held a staff made from the bones of a human arm. The hand at the end twitched and curled like a wizard casting spells. It was pointed at Buzz.

"What's that?" Austin said, skidding to a stop behind them.

"Owen Ren Leng, Necromancer," the Chinese wizard said. "Bearer of the Withered Arm of the Seventh King of Hell." And he touched the pointing finger of the staff to the street.

"Of course you are," Austin said, and Austin and JT both shot him. JT drew the pistol he'd forgotten about and, two-handed, emptied the clip into the necromancer. Austin fired his last two arrows. Bullets and arrows all punched right through him, holes in the front, holes in the back, but all he bled was tiny bits of shredded paper, and that didn't seem to bother him one bit. As they fired away, green mist boiled up from the ground where the Withered Arm touched, and slithered toward them.

The tendrils slid past them, beneath the net of flame Austin had created, to the bodies that littered the street. They slid into noses, mouths, ears, and any other hole they found. Dead eyes filled with green light, and the corpses rose, jerky like marionettes with an unskilled puppeteer. The zombies shambled toward them. They passed through the net of fire, shredding it into a shower of sparks. Some of the zombies burst into flame, but they kept walking, human torches lighting the street orange and filling it with the smell of burnt pork. Dead mouths opened. Teeth erupted into fangs. Hands rose and nails sharpened to claws.

"What the fuck did you steal?" JT shouted at Buzz. "Everyone off the street!" and he bullrushed them all to the side of the road. Drones Three through Six came blazing through, one after the other, strobing the street with gunfire. The bullets chewed up pavement and blew bodies to smithereens, but the zombies didn't care, and there were so many of them, so many more than there should have been.

And Austin was in the middle of it all. Knives out, he rushed the necromancer. The necromancer whirled into the air and came down behind Austin, his bone staff sweeping. Austin leapt the staff, made his own impossible midair spin, knives all a blur, and ribbons of embroidered cloth fluttered away. But even with the necromancer occupied, the zombies kept coming.

Buzz tried to bolt, but JT held him back. "Just a few seconds," he said.

The necromancer shrieked and swirled through the air around Austin, parrying Austin's strikes. Then the staff's skeletal hand simply grabbed one of Austin's blades. It went white with frost, and Austin dropped it, cursing and shaking his hand like he'd been burnt.

And from down the hill: headlights high above ground, coming in fast. Austin leapt. JT's truck slammed into the hovering necromancer with a sickening *whump*. Broken jade scattered over the street like shrapnel. A cloud of hell money burst from the robes as if that was all the necromancer had been. Empty, the robes swept beneath the truck. Stamped paper joss swirled angrily in the back draft. The truck kept right on going, smashing zombies beneath wheels the size of elephants. It screeched to a stop, backed up and did it again.

"Stop messing around, JT!" Austin yelled from the truck bed where he'd landed. "Let's go!"

"That's your truck?" Buzz said awestruck as they all ran, dodging broken-up zombies. Even ruined and smashed, they hissed and clawed and dragged themselves across the pavement toward them.

"I made it from scratch."

"Gods help us all," Victor said.

They climbed the ladders into the cab. Austin stayed in the back. JT threw the truck into gear, and they barreled down the street. And the last thing JT saw of Telegraph Hill were three SFPD fliers up in the air bathing the carnage behind them in stark white spotlights, while the silhouettes of a score of broken zombies reached up to them, hungry. JT shook his head in sad disbelief.

What had Buzz and Austin stolen that had been worth so much?

CHAPTER SEVEN

F ive years ago, someone had broken up with JT. Today, JT couldn't even remember the guy's name. Paul? Doug? One of the four-letter names. But, back then, it had felt like the world had fallen apart— again—the way it always did when men decided he wasn't the one.

So a moody JT had jumped the curb and parked his truck on the edge of the headlands overlooking Black Sands Beach, and he and Austin had sat on the back gate and watched the city lights to the south go hazy and the Pacific waters darken. They drank beer out of plastic. JT sat hunch-shouldered, and Austin leaned against him, his shoulder warm. They'd been sitting for fifteen minutes when JT had looked at Austin and said, "Consolation sex?"

Austin tapped his bottle against JT's and gave him a sad, sympathetic smile. "Whatever you need. But you gotta do what I say."

JT shrugged, sure. Just then, probably he'd have done anything Austin had asked if only to feel loved.

Austin told him to strip and lie down on his stomach on the blanket they'd laid out in the bed of the truck. It hadn't been very comfortable—the blanket was warm, but it wasn't enough padding to keep the corrugated plastic of the truck bed from pressing into him. He pushed his cock and balls down so they weren't smashed underneath him.

Austin had good strong hands. JT had always thought so. They were all tendon and veins and white scar tissue. He laid them on JT's shoulders and didn't move. He left them there so long, JT started to ask him what he was doing, and Austin said, "Shush. Do what I say, right?"

"You didn't say anything."

"I said shush."

So JT had turned his face down into the blanket and gave a good long sigh and waited for whatever Austin was going to do. He'd expected a fucking like Austin usually gave him: bent over the truck walls, or hanging upside-down off the gate, or against the half-rotting and rickety stairs that led down to the private little cove they knew of, stairs that only got replaced when someone broke them and nearly died from the fall. That was the kind of fucking JT and Austin did. That wasn't what Austin was doing to him now.

Austin kneaded his fingers into JT's shoulders and neck, working him slowly, like he was a stubborn kind of clay. Austin's thumbs traced the seams between muscles. His fingers found cramped knots and kneaded them flat. They slid up his neck to his temples. They traced down his sides. They lifted his feet and pressed deep into his arches. It hurt like Austin was breaking them. It brought tears to his eyes.

"Where did you learn—"

"I said shush." And Austin kept on.

Somewhere in all that, Austin stripped. JT didn't know when. But he felt Austin's skin against his own, hard and hot as fresh-poured steel. And when Austin moved onto some other part of JT (Austin's cock dragging lightly behind), JT's skin cooled in the evening air. He shivered and his skin pimpled in gooseflesh everywhere.

Austin trickled beer over JT. It ran cold down the cleft of JT's spine between fans of muscle and pooled in the small of his back above the crack of his ass. Austin lapped the pool dry and poured more. It tickled, and Austin's tongue was so soothing all over him that he didn't know whether he still wanted to fuck or would rather have slept the deepest sleep he'd ever had. He lost track of time. Maybe he had fallen asleep. So exactly when Austin's fingers finally found JT's ass, he couldn't say. But they were there now, and JT thought Austin was going to push a finger or thumb inside him, but he didn't. He teased and massaged and pulled at his hole until JT was good and ready, and then Austin pushed his way in, all the way in, and the warmth of Austin's body settled on him.

The night had been cold and the breeze off the ocean wet and smelling of salt, but JT had felt warm and spread out, taken apart and ready to be re-assembled into a man. And so Austin had done. He fucked JT slower and longer than JT had ever been fucked in his life (or ever fucked since).

Austin's glamour threaded through him: lust and violence. JT felt it build, felt his blood respond to Austin the way it always did: the rising need to fight, to add pain to the mix, the almost irresistible urge to throw Austin off him, to hold the elf down and show him how fucking was really done. He fought it the way he always did (and always he lost the fight). His hands twitched, and he balled them into fists and his knuckles went white.

Austin did what he'd never done before. He took JT's balled-up fists and he pried them open and pressed his thumbs into JT's palms, and pulled on his fingers, and kissed them until the need to hit something subsided. And all the while Austin never stopped fucking, never stopped impaling JT slowly, never stopped sliding his cock at that perfect angle to rub JT's insides. Every time the need returned, Austin's hands and lips were there to defuse it. Each time. Every time. Austin kept him balanced on the edge of need forever. It felt like madness breaking through. The world went hazy and timeless. Austin's hands and lips were everywhere, brushing him quiet.

"Is that magic?" JT said, nearly in tears, not knowing how much longer he could endure this.

Austin kept fucking, slow as planets moving, slow as lava spilling. "Yep," he whispered. "I have a magic dick, didn't you know?"

"I need one of those."

"They only made the one."

He felt Austin come. Slow as Austin was moving, he felt Austin's cock throb and the warmth fill his ass. Austin's come was always hot. JT could always feel it. Austin's breath shivered, and his fingers tightened a bit on JT's arms. And that was all the sign of Austin's coming there was. Austin didn't stop.

"JT?" Austin said. How many times he had said it, JT didn't know, he was so lost in the haze. He barely felt like a physical thing anymore. "JT?"

"Yes?" JT said, nothing more than a hiss of air.

Austin whispered in his ear, "You're worth being loved. One of these days, someone's going to realize that, and they're going to love you. Say it for me and I'll let you come. Say, 'Someone's gonna love me. I'm worth being loved.'"

JT couldn't say it. He didn't believe it, and just now, he couldn't lie.

"Say it, JT."

"I'm worth— I'm worth— Someone's gonna—"

Someone's gonna love you.

Buzz was huddled in the dark near the truck's passenger door, shaggy copper-brown hair everywhere. He looked asleep. As cars passed them and headlight glare drew across the cab, JT could see Buzz's eyes were closed and his lips pursed as if he was dreaming of kissing. Buzz had asked for access to the truck's network, so JT had given it to him. Buzz's mind in the truck's computer alongside his was even more of a presence than his physical body there in the cab. It felt as if Buzz were standing just behind him, almost touching but not. And if JT just leaned back, there Buzz would be, solid as flesh.

Somehow Buzz kept it all quiet—no SFPD pursuit or Pacifica Bureau of Investigation requests made—and they slid across the Bay Bridge with no pursuit. It was a two-hour drive up I-80 with no magway to Tahoe, where they'd rendezvous with 3djinn and hand off the data block. They'd get there just after sunrise.

Austin lounged in the truck bed in the space left by Drone Two's absence. It had to be uncomfortable wedged in back there like that, but of course Austin didn't look uncomfortable. He looked far more comfortable than JT, Buzz, and Victor all smashed into the cab, especially with Victor sitting in the middle.

—*Hey*, Buzz sent to JT. It didn't sound like speech. It sounded like JT's own verbalized thoughts, though with an alien quality, a tone or timbre or color that wasn't JT's own. The alien quality was intentional, placed there by the translation protocol so that the receiver didn't develop paranoia.

—*Hey.*

—*Open ports AB12 through AC12.*

—*You want to feel the air pressure in my tires?*

—*Not the truck's ports. Yours.*

—*Oh.* AB12 through AC12 were the ports used for simstim transmissions. JT kept those ports firewalled with exceptions only to integrate with the machines he needed. JT didn't open them. —*If you wanted to hack my mind, could you do it?*

—*That's disgusting.*

—*But could you?*

A long pause. Darkness outside, nothing to measure the time between question and answer. —*Maybe. Probably, yeah. But I wouldn't ever—*

Probably, yeah. Probably, yeah, Buzz could take over JT's mind and drop him into a hallucination so profound it would damage JT's psyche permanently. Probably, yeah, Buzz could fry him the way that Roan had been fried. And, yes, it had probably been someone like Buzz who had killed her. Probably, yeah, Buzz could delete JT's memories or add a few of his own and maybe JT wouldn't even know it. Probably, yeah, Buzz could make JT think he was in love just like Austin's glamour did.

JT added Buzz to the exception list.

At first, JT couldn't quite tell what Buzz had sent him. A pleasant sensation, sure, but strangely disconnected from any other sense. Then the pressure grew on his lips, and something pushed past them into his mouth, warm and soft. Buzz was kissing him. Or Buzz was transmitting the sensations of being kissed directly into JT's brain. Nothing parted JT's lips, though he felt Buzz's tongue. Nothing pressed his lips flat, though he felt Buzz press into him. And there was no taste at all coded into the simstim packet.

Then the sensation faded until all that was left was tingling in JT's lips and tongue.

—*Thank you for saving me,* Buzz sent.

—*You're welcome. That was nice.*

—*Was it? I wrote that.*

—*You've been writing simstims?*

—*New hobby. Just messing around. You on autopilot?*

—*Yeah.*

—*Good. Lean back. 'Cause I wrote some other things too.*

That consolation sex, five years ago?

JT had edited his memories same as everyone's ever done. He'd taken safety scissors and cut out all the parts that hurt too much. (And sometimes on the reverse side of those pages had been the best parts of other memories, everything mangled now.)

Austin had whispered in his ear, "You're worth being loved. One of these days, someone's going to realize that, and they're going to love you. Say it for me and I'll let you come. Say, 'I'm worth being loved.'" And Austin fucked him and JT vibrated beneath him, balanced on the edge of an ecstasy that felt like madness. "Say it, JT."

"I'm worth being loved."

JT had come forever, it felt like. Like he'd always been coming and would never stop. He whimpered and clawed at the blanket and his cock and balls pumped and throbbed. But Austin's kisses branding his neck and shoulders, Austin's fingers entwining in his, holding his hands so tightly, he wouldn't allow himself to remember. And minutes later, hours later, years later, it seemed, they'd rolled apart and faced one another. They were still holding hands, and neither let go.

On the blanket between them was a white puddle the size of Lake Erie. Austin broke into a grin, like all that come had been his. "Christ, I'm amazing." And then he grabbed JT and kissed him hard. "Someone's gonna love you." And maybe you'd think that Austin was teasing because that's what Austin did, but the way Austin's eyes had looked into JT's, JT knew Austin wasn't teasing. Those words might have been the most sincere words Austin had ever said to him.

Why can't it be you? JT had thought with the force of thought that was almost but not quite speech. *Why can't you love me? Why can't it be you?* He'd untangled his fingers from Austin's, the last time he'd ever dared to hold Austin's hand.

The cutting-room floor of JT's mind was littered with memories in Austin-shaped pieces.

Austin had forgotten how much he liked watching JT sweat.

North of the Sacramento sprawl, they had pulled off for a battery exchange. The unmanned, sketchy-looking cinder-block building, tucked in a clearing amid fir trees one K off the highway, was nothing much more than a restroom and shower. There was a vending machine too, but the Plexiglas front of it had been shot away and all the candy bars had been stolen. Surrounding the building were picnic tables. Behind it was a metal rack with slots for fifty or so batteries. Lights next to half of them said green; the other half said amber. Cables led from the rack to a half-acre sun farm that filled the rest of the clearing.

The exchange worked on the honor system: replace what you take. It didn't seem like that should work to Austin. It seemed like someone should just take all the batteries the same way someone had taken all the candy bars. Austin was hungry. Someday he would find the guy who'd stolen all those candy bars.

JT's truck ran on batteries and fuel cells, both. His drones ran on batteries and recharged from the truck. After the fight on Telegraph Hill, everything was nearly tapped out. So JT was pulling the batteries from his truck, slotting them into empty charger slots, and replacing them with fully charged ones. It wasn't a difficult task, but the truck was high off the ground; the batteries weighed about twelve kilos apiece, and though the sun had only just risen, it was already ninety-five in the valley.

Buzz was sitting cross-legged in the truck trying to contact 3djinn. Victor—without any warning—had grotesquely popped one of the silver eyes from his head and begun polishing it with a black silk handkerchief embroidered with runes. He didn't cover the gaping socket and no one wanted to be near him. Nebraska, invisible to everyone but Austin, was out hunting for rocks. And Austin sat on a sun-blasted picnic table and watched JT sweat.

JT was trying to straighten a bent rail in one of the slots near the ground. Bending over like that stretched his jeans over the most perfect ass Austin had ever seen. JT's chopped-up flannel shirt (way too hot for this weather here) pulled up and his jeans buckled out in a V, exposing the small of his back and the waistband of a pair of blue underwear. A bead of sweat ran down his spine to the waistband where it soaked into a spreading darker blue.

"When did you start wearing underwear?" Austin said.

"When I got tired of walking into investor meetings and having everyone stare at my junk. I don't know how people wear them."

Other people aren't hung like a horse, Austin thought. JT didn't like comments on his size.

"They're uncomfortable as hell," JT said. "What's so hard about making a pair of underwear that fits orcs? It ain't particle physics; it's fashion. Are you staring at my ass?" JT stood, hiked up his jeans with his thumbs, and tugged his shirt down. But he kept his ass turned to Austin and only looked over his shoulder.

JT was flirting. It was practically a goddamn miracle.

"I was until you just ruined it. Bend over again."

JT gave him a sly grin. "What if I'm done here?"

"Then show me what to break so you can fix it again."

"Lucky you, I don't have to pretend." And JT bent over and went back to trying to fix the bracket. And when his jeans rode down and his shirt rode up, he didn't try to fix that.

Through his jeans, JT's ass was just the right combination of muscle and smoothness. Hard thighs stretched the denim tight, and arms glistened green under the sun, straining against bent steel. His lug-soled work boots ground in gravel. When JT stood and whipped off his ball cap and wiped his brow like a hero from some old simflick, Austin couldn't help but smile. JT snorted a laugh, all bashful now. "You enjoying yourself?"

"You're in a better mood."

JT glanced at Buzz. "I suppose I am."

That little glance was like a cold knife to Austin's gut. And Austin had been stabbed in the gut plenty of times, so, yeah, it really did feel just like that. JT turned back to his repair project, though why he bothered, Austin didn't know. He supposed it was some other part of the honor system that ran this place: you saw something broken, you fixed it.

JT said, "Why you still got that rock? It's just junk."

Austin looked down at his hands and, goddamn, there it was: limestone with a malachite stripe. He hadn't even noticed he'd taken it out and been fiddling with it, rolling it over his fingers like it was part of some magic trick. "Yeah, it's just junk." He rolled it in his hand a bit more, drew back to fling it as far as he fucking could, then palmed it and dropped it back into his little satchel with the only other one he had left. It was stupid to throw away magic, wasn't it?

He didn't want to watch JT work anymore. He jumped down from the table. "I need to go find some more rocks."

"You think they're going to keep after us?"

"Until we get the Blue Unicorn to 3djinn, they ain't gonna stop."

"You ever gonna tell me what this Blue Unicorn thing is?"

"Buzz," Austin shouted. "Buzz!" And Buzz finally came back to earth from whatever network he'd been communing with. "Get that thing ready. It's time to see what we got," and Austin tromped off into the woods to find Nebraska, the only bit of sanity the world had left.

"I need root access," Buzz said.

"No," JT said, watching Austin disappear into the woods. Austin was pissed again, JT knew it, but he couldn't figure why. If anything, it should have been JT pissed at Austin, not the other way around. But he wasn't pissed anymore, was he? However many lies Austin might have told, Buzz had still needed saving, Austin had been right about that. And reconnecting with Buzz, that was worth putting up with Austin, wasn't it?

"Your truck's system isn't configured to handle the Blue Unicorn. If I'm going to show her to you, I need to change a few things."

"No, it's my truck."

"You trusted me to send sims straight into your head, but you won't trust me with your truck?"

He had a point, there. They'd passed a good half hour of the drive with Buzz trying to get a reaction out of JT: a barrage of virtual kisses on JT's lips and neck, strokes along JT's body, a tug at one nipple, and finally a tentative stroke around the head of JT's cock that had made JT growl loud enough for Victor to give him a worried look. Buzz had snickered at that. JT had mumbled some excuse about traffic to Victor and sent to Buzz, —*Give me some of those programs. We'll see how you like it.*

—*Hell no. Write your own. And if you didn't like it, you could have always closed off those ports.*

—*Oh yeah?* And JT closed them.

Buzz had laughed aloud, which had earned his own look from Victor.

"Fine, I'll trade you. Access for access," JT said.

"I ain't dumb enough to let you in my head." Buzz had one deep dimple when he grinned broad like he was. In the morning light, his hair showed copper, the same color as his freckles. He was the cutest damn thing JT had ever seen.

"Not the access I'm thinking of." JT put an oversized hand on the back of Buzz's neck and steered him behind the cinder-block building where no one would see.

JT pushed Buzz against the wall of the exchange. That sweat and nervous scent on Buzz, that smell was fucking heaven. But nervous or not, Buzz didn't flinch or pull away or whimper. He leaned his head back and exposed his neck to JT, and that earned a low growl. JT lapped the sweat from Buzz, hungrier for him than he'd ever been.

But maybe Buzz's nerves weren't all because of JT. "It ain't over, is it? I mean there's more coming, ain't there? Maybe this ain't a good time."

JT sucked at the curve where Buzz's neck met his shoulder. Buzz tasted salty, sharp, and metallic. "It's a perfect time."

"Last time you said that, we got shot at."

JT ran a hand over Buzz's crotch. Buzz was hard. JT dropped to his knees and looked up at him. Buzz looked nervously over at the tree line where Austin had gone. "What if Austin—"

"What about it?" It wouldn't be the first time Austin had seen JT blow a guy. Austin only cared who JT fucked so far as it gave him ammunition for teasing JT later. And considering how Austin had reacted before to the idea of JT and Buzz together, he kind of hoped the elf reappeared at just the right moment. Imagine the look on Austin's face when JT licked Buzz's come off his tusks.

He tugged Buzz's pants and boxers down to his knees. Buzz's hair was copper orange just like he'd said. He was cut and his cock was pale pink, the head a shade darker. His nuts were tight and unshaven. JT turned his ball cap backward, then nuzzled at them, rubbing his face in Buzz's crotch, inhaling Buzz's tang deep like it was oxygen. JT tried to be careful as he could—even orcs got nervous when tusks got near their nuts—but there was bound to be a scratch or a nip no matter how careful he was. Buzz would just have to decide whether it was worth it or not, and JT was determined to make sure it was.

He liked the feeling of Buzz's nuts on his cheek and Buzz's smooth-as-silk cock brushing his forehead, his cheeks, his lips. He sucked at the tender inside of Buzz's thighs: right, then left. He kissed Buzz above his thatch of orange hair. Buzz's cock brushed along JT's neck as he did. And then he took Buzz into his mouth in one long suck.

Orc mouths were bigger than a human's and Buzz fit JT like he was made to be there. All the way down, JT's nose in curly hairs, and the tip of Buzz pressed lightly against the back of JT's throat, just enough to tickle and make him want to swallow. JT ran his tongue back and forth over the underside of Buzz. He swallowed and sucked good and hard, then pulled away until it was only Buzz's head between JT's lips, and then he sucked even harder. Buzz started whispering random bits of nonsense ecstasy—curses and half words and sounds that weren't anything—and JT knew he was doing something Buzz hadn't felt before.

—*Open up, JT*, came Buzz knocking at JT's mind. JT opened the ports like he'd done in the truck, and Buzz swept him with simulated touches, and even in the valley heat—a hundred degrees now—JT's body went gooseflesh everywhere and he shivered. It felt like so many men—three, a dozen, he didn't know—all stroking his body softly, along his arms, his chest, his flanks, the inside of his legs, long feather-touch strokes. He felt a hand on the back of his head, and it was a moment before he realized it was a real hand. Buzz held JT's head lightly, rubbing his fingers against the stubbly hair.

—*That's it*, JT sent to Buzz, not wanting to take Buzz out of his mouth, not even for a second. —*Show me what you want. Fuck my mouth the way you want.* JT put one hand on Buzz's ass and another on the small of his back to brace himself better.

But Buzz just groaned and leaned against the wall and sent, —*Just like that, JT, just like that.* So JT kept it up, sucking, licking, swallowing, gliding his tongue around Buzz, until finally Buzz's hips started to twitch forward.

Buzz's sim strokes switched up, and JT's nuts started to tingle. JT growled and purred at the sensation, not knowing whether it was his own or something Buzz was doing, and Buzz sighed as the vibration traveled along his cock, and his other hand tangled into JT's thick bangs.

Pull my head down on you, JT begged without sending. *Pull me down by my hair. Down by my goddamn ears. By anything. Take my mouth. Fuck me. Fuck me, Buzz.* And JT sucked furiously. All of him was set on fire. His cock pinched painfully in that goddamn pair of underwear and too-tight jeans, and it wouldn't take nothing at all to make JT explode. Just the right strong touch. And though Buzz flinched from the nick of a tusk, his hips kept twitching with need. But it wasn't fucking, it wasn't movement enough.

Austin would have fucked him. Austin would have used JT's mouth until JT's jaw hurt. Austin would have known what JT wanted and needed. And, for a moment, it nagged at him that Buzz wasn't as rough as JT liked. But that thought never got more than half-formed.

The simulated touches went like static all over. Buzz whispered curses and JT's name, then his cock throbbed twice and come flooded JT's mouth. And now, finally, Buzz's hand twisted painfully in JT's hair, and Buzz forced JT's head down so he had no choice but to swallow while Buzz bucked into him. And JT loved it, he loved it. The taste of Buzz was like Buzz's sweat: salt and metallic tang sliding down JT's throat, slick and warm, and what didn't go down filled JT's mouth. Even when Buzz's spasms stopped and his hands eased their grip and he slid a few centimeters down the cinder-block wall gasping, JT held him there, not wanting to give up the taste of him.

The truck's cyberlink was quiet, and neither of them moved but for heaving chests. Reluctantly, JT sat back on his heels. He let Buzz go only very slowly, licking him clean as he went. Buzz's cock was bright pink, visibly scraped in a couple of places. It had to be sore. Probably JT shouldn't have gotten so crazy, Buzz's first time with an orc and all. Probably JT had just scared the hell of out him and that was the last bit of Buzz he'd ever get. But all Buzz said was, "Wow."

Relieved, JT stood and kissed him. The salt of Buzz's lips mingled with the lingering taste of his come.

"You feeling focused, now?" Buzz asked.

"Pretty damn focused." He tucked Buzz back in his jeans and zipped and buttoned them for him.

Buzz glanced down. JT's jeans were dark with damp. Buzz smiled, "I got you off."

"Nah, I just get excited like that. You got me off, you'd have known it."

"Well, shit."

JT smiled, put his arms around him, and kissed him again. "So you owe me."

Buzz seemed to like that idea. "So you ready to find out why all the trouble? Access for access, baby, that was the deal. Hook me up."

Following Buzz back to the truck, JT cast a glance at the woods and made a show of wiping his chin. But, damn it, Austin wasn't there to see.

CHAPTER EIGHT

Nebraska slipped away to wherever he went when he hid from everyone, and Austin emerged from the woods into the fuel exchange clearing.

Victor the Wizard's eye was back in his head, and JT and Buzz were standing together near the ladder of the passenger side of the truck. They weren't talking and both had their eyes closed. "They haven't finished yet?" he asked Victor.

Victor turned to him. His eyes were even freakier than before. One was dark and tarnished; the other, bright. It made him look unbalanced. "They've only just started."

"I've been gone for twenty minutes."

"Yes. Well. I'm glad we have a few minutes. I was hoping we could talk."

"Yeah? About what?"

"I wanted to apologize for what I said earlier . . . about wanting to study you."

Austin scowled at the wizard. He didn't like the topic, and he didn't like apologies.

Victor misread the scowl as a demand for more instead of a demand to stop and kept on talking. "One hears stories about children disappearing off the streets, elven and orc children, sick experiments, but it's hard to know whether these stories are real or urban legends. One hopes they are urban legends. It was bad enough the way the zero generation of your people was treated; no one wants to believe—"

"Yeah, that's nice, thanks."

"It's science. Science consumes the soul. I'm pleased I forsook that world and became a wizard."

Austin stared in disbelief and wrestled between the urge to set the record straight and change the subject. "For your information, JT and I weren't taken as children. We were taken when our team was killed two years ago. They got killed; we got captured. And we weren't taken by scientists; we were taken by wizards."

Victor paled and blinked his mismatched eyes.

"So, apology accepted. Now shut the hell up. What the fuck is taking so long?" He waved toward JT and Buzz standing there.

And then the details sunk in. Why had it taken them so long to start? Why were JT and Buzz standing like that? So close to each other, turned to each other like that? With JT's hand twitching like that, like JT wanted to touch Buzz . . . or maybe in cyberspace JT already was. "They had sex."

Victor coughed and looked at the ground.

"Are they still having sex?"

"They don't appear to be."

"Virtual sex."

"I really couldn't say. That world is barred to me."

But one glance at JT told Austin they weren't doing that. Some things the orc couldn't hide.

"You know we're in the middle of a dangerous mission?" Austin said.

"I . . . am aware, yes," Victor said.

"That kind of behavior, that's irresponsible."

"I didn't feel it was my role to—"

"You two!" Austin strode toward JT and Buzz. "Do I need to turn a hose on you two?"

"Austin's back," Buzz grumbled to JT. Was that disappointment Austin heard in the ungrateful twerp's voice? And JT's little chuckle didn't help one bit.

"You're right, Austin's back," Austin said. "Austin's goddamn back and ain't going anywhere. Now let's get this started."

There were disadvantages to working with humans and orcs, and the stink was one of them. The four of them were crammed into the cab of JT's truck with the AC blasting, but that only went so far. Austin was wedged against the passenger-side door, Victor straddled the middle, and Buzz might as well have been sitting in JT's lap. Wasn't that just fucking adorable?

Buzz's eyes were open and kept focusing on things no one else but he and JT could see. JT's eyes were closed. He kept flinching or grimacing as if whatever Buzz was doing to the network of his truck physically hurt him. Buzz talked while he worked, like whatever he was doing was nothing more difficult than walking and chewing bubble gum.

Austin sat there and glared at Buzz and JT and thought vague dark thoughts.

Buzz was saying, "So the Electric Dragon Triad contacts me, says they have this ghost problem, and right off I'm thinking like you guys are: you got a ghost, you find a necromancer or a holy man, not a hacker. But they didn't mean that kind of ghost. They meant a ghost in their network, an AI fragment."

He paused and no one said anything, which apparently was not the reaction he wanted. "An AI fragment," he repeated. "No one knows? Really? This is what happens when you get everyday magic: no one learns about technology anymore. An AI fragment is what you get sometimes when an artificial intelligence breaks, or when it's forming and it gets a trait it doesn't want; it sheds it. It's like glaciers and icebergs. Pieces of its mind break off and go floating around cyberspace and sometimes they get washed up on beaches and people find them. The fragments are barely sentient, usually just a clump of bad memories, and they're kind of obsessive. So: 'ghosts.'"

"Whales," Victor said.

"What?"

"Whales. Whales used to get washed up on beaches, not icebergs."

Buzz's eyes focused on Victor. He blinked a couple of times. "What are you talking about?"

"Never mind."

JT cracked a smile. One of JT's huge arms was propped across the back of the seat behind Buzz. He shifted so that his fingers brushed against Buzz's hair. *Real slick*, Austin thought. *Not subtle at all.* Austin tried to imagine JT and Buzz having sex. What would they have done?

Handjobs? Blowjobs? Had they actually fucked? Austin couldn't imagine Buzz on top (like Buzz would know what to do with someone like JT under him), and he couldn't imagine Buzz on bottom (like Buzz would be walking after JT finished up). Austin couldn't imagine any of it.

Victor nodded at the data cube in Buzz's hand. "So that's what you've stolen? This ghost? This must be very valuable to go to all this trouble: my apartment ruined, a gunfight over the city . . ."

"They're valuable to some people." Buzz's eyes lost focus again as he went back to work. "We've got no idea how many unregistered AI's there are out there—not even 3djinn has a good idea—and a ghost can contain all kinds of fragmented, recoverable data about the original entity. So it's kind of a big deal to catch one." Buzz blinked as he pulled out of the truck's cyberspace. "That's it, JT. We're ready."

But Buzz didn't slot the data block just yet. "So the Electric Dragon Triad, they're behind a lot of shit: drugs, of course. Arms dealing. The slave trade. And porn."

"Pornography isn't illegal," Victor said.

"The kind they make is." Buzz didn't elaborate, but they all knew what he meant. He asked JT, "You ever jacked an elf porn sim?"

Austin smiled, satisfied. "He's never needed to."

Buzz went red as neon. He looked away from JT and shifted uncomfortably.

JT stopped playing with Buzz's hair. The green tips of his ears tinged red like he was embarrassed, but the look on his face was anything but. He glared at Austin. "Maybe I needed to more than you think."

Austin didn't know what that might mean, but he didn't see any reason why anyone should be embarrassed or pissed, either one. Everyone knew JT and Austin had fucked. Hell, most of the world thought they'd been in some kind of relationship.

"Virtual sex," Victor sneered. Magic and tech didn't mix, which meant Austin and Victor couldn't wear the implants that allowed simulated stimuli, including high-end pornography. Austin could pop on a pair of VR glasses and at least got the first-person, 3-D effect, but Victor probably refused to wear even those. Probably, if

Victor wanted porn, he just looked at still images or read print stories, the poor bastard. Probably Victor the Wizard was a virgin and told everyone his virginity was a source of his power.

"Well, it all sucks," Buzz said. "I mean, it isn't any better than human porn sim. It's the glamour. Everyone always talks about elf glamour and how amazing it makes the sex—"

"It isn't all that," JT mumbled.

"You haven't had an elf?" Austin said to Buzz. "I should introduce you to an elf."

That first time for Austin and JT had been JT's first time with an elf. And what had started as a nice, casual blowjob had gone a whole lot more wild once Austin's glamour got hold of JT. JT had given Austin a throat-fucking that left Austin so sore he'd spent two days whispering. It had been amazing. Imagine Buzz taking all of JT down his throat like Austin had done? No way. So it had to have been handjobs while Austin was gone into the woods, and handjobs hardly even counted as sex. That was just saying hello. And somehow Austin felt better about the whole thing already.

"I'll find you an elf," he told Buzz.

Buzz ignored them all and, to his credit, didn't miss a beat. "—but you can't record it or re-create it. It's magic. They always try to code in something that's supposed to fake an elf's glamour—pull certain memories out of the jacker and lay them over the scene, add in experiences that are supposedly universally erotic—but it's never right. There's a lot of money for the person who figures it out. A whole lot of money."

"No one can figure it out," Victor said. "You can't figure out what is impossible. A computer cannot cast spells, cameras cannot see spirits, and a glamour cannot be recorded or coded. You may as well say that someday mathematicians will learn how to make one plus one equal three."

"That's what I would have said two weeks ago," Buzz said. He held up the data cube.

"You're telling me that ghost has a glamour?" JT said.

"Yes."

JT and Victor started to argue, but Buzz cut them off. "I'm almost done with the story, and then you can jack it yourself." He turned to

Victor and Austin. "Even without the hardware, you are going to feel it—you just won't be able to see the ghost." Victor looked doubtful, but Buzz continued. "So, end of the story: The Triad offered me a job to figure out how the ghost worked. Reverse engineer it."

JT said, "Because once they knew how to do it, they could put glamour on pornography. And you fucking said yes? Those people are fucking animals, Buzz. Do you know what they do? Do you know what kind of porn they're making? It ain't just people having fun, and it sure as hell ain't a romance!"

"What was I supposed to do, JT? I was this far away from the most important discovery since the Awakening: how to break down the barrier between magic and technology. And you think I should have left that to a fucking Triad? It was right in front of me, and all I needed to do was work with some bad people for a while. Don't tell me you've never worked for bad people. You've spent your entire life working for bad people!"

The AC fans were a loud whine in the quiet. JT shifted. He lowered his arm across the back of the seat again so he was touching Buzz's shoulder. "So how did Austin get involved?" he said.

"I called him. I called Austin and asked him to help me steal her. I told you it was my idea. Once I saw what the Blue Unicorn was, I couldn't leave her there. Not with them. Not knowing what they'd do to her. So I broke my contract. Jesus, I'm the first 3djinn ever to break a contract, I think. They are going to be so pissed."

"You said ghosts were barely sentient," JT said. "Why are you talking like this thing's a person all of a sudden?"

Buzz shot a glance to Austin.

This was it. For two years now, Austin had been looking for this proof. Proof JT had been wrong to leave. Proof JT had been kidding himself when he thought he could make a normal life. Proof JT should come back and the two of them—just the two of them—should be a team like they had been before everything had gone bad. If this didn't convince JT to come back, nothing would. "Just play it."

Buzz whined, "Austin, I don't think . . ."

"Just play it."

Buzz sighed. "Jack in, JT. You ain't gonna like this." And Buzz slapped the data cube into the port on JT's truck.

It felt like a séance JT had once joined in, the four of them squeezed so close into his truck, waiting for something to reach out from cyberspace and touch their minds. All apprehensive quiet, all but the fans blowing cold air on high.

JT fell into the truck's cyberspace. It was neither light nor dark. It was neutral nothing, electric gray.

JT never bothered with avatars much. He'd never cared what he looked like in here. For JT, cyberspace was a network interface, not a social space; he rarely needed an avatar. Buzz, on the other hand, looked just like Buzz, not even the slightest alteration to what he looked like out there. He was sitting cross-legged like some kind of yogi. —*Open up*, Buzz sent, meaning the sim ports.

—*That's not safe, not with that thing in here. And I won't need those ports open if it has a glamour. I don't need to be here at all.*

—*C'mon, open up.*

JT did. He felt Buzz's fingers intertwine with his. —*My world. My turn to keep you safe.*

JT wished he had the program so that Buzz could feel JT's hand the way JT could feel his. They sat there holding hands, waiting as if for the sun to rise.

Cactus flowers. —*Cactus flowers.* "I smell flowers," JT said aloud. "Weed," Buzz said.

"The sea," Victor said.

A thrill shot through JT. If Victor smelled something, could it be this was true?

"I don't smell anything," Austin said.

"You will," Buzz said.

JT told Buzz he was going to drop out.

—*Okay, but come back. I want you to see it.*

JT dropped back into real space. Even without a direct connection to the truck's cyberspace, he could still smell flowers. The scent grew more complex. Not just flowers, but dust and hot wind.

JT fell back in to watercolors, warm horizontal stripes: yellows, oranges, and reds. A blue unicorn chasing butterflies. The unicorn was stark and exact against the smeary watercolor backdrop. It charged, all piss and vinegar, and tried to spear monarchs on its horn, and then it lost interest and simply trotted around. Yellow-orange-red became a mountainside. "The Painted Desert."

"Twin Peaks," Buzz said.

It was true. It was an honest-to-goddess glamour somehow coded into a broken-off piece of some AI. The glamour took the simulated stimuli and somehow made them more than real. It spoke to each of them individually and stirred up old memories and daydreams and nightmares and made the world vivid, lush, and seductive. How was this possible?

Austin said, "Winchester Mountain."

"You can see it?"

"No." Austin's voice was soft and distant. "But I can smell the wind now and the snow, and I know that smell. Buzz, you found her."

And then the sensoria crashed down on JT like a thunderstorm.

A thousand fragments of memory like holographic glass: each containing the whole, yet still broken ragged. So many images and sounds, JT couldn't sort them all, and it was all just sound and fury. Except that it hurt. The pieces of it grazed against his mind, and JT couldn't flinch away from it because the Blue Unicorn was everywhere.

It was raining.

Mounted police. What city was this? Seattle. Except the policeman was riding a blue unicorn and its silver hooves struck sparks from asphalt. The policeman's visor reflected them when he looked down.

"She's my sister," Austin said. He was fourteen maybe and beautiful as sin. Roan was brown-skinned and Austin was pale as funeral lilies, but in this day and age, what did that mean? Nothing—same way Buzz and Austin could both be Irish and two different species entirely.

The policeman didn't seem to care who was related to who. "Move along."

In puddles, Austin and Roan reflected. Austin and Roan in Seattle. Austin and Roan in San Francisco. Austin and Roan in an alpine wilderness. Blue Unicorns everywhere. JT couldn't tell if the Unicorn was a memory or a daydream. He wasn't sure if there were any unicorns. When the elves and orcs had Awakened, had horses Awakened too? When Austin had been born, had a unicorn also been born somewhere? When JT was born, was there a nightmare born, smoke-maned and breathing fire? Had ranchers drowned their mutant horses the way some humans had their mutant children?

—*Buzz?* JT was starting to panic. This was not just a glamour. The images were coming too fast, alien thoughts and memories flung at him like a poltergeist, furious and throwing anything it could find. "Buzz!" JT shouted aloud. He couldn't feel Buzz's hand in his anymore. "Buzz! Where are you?"

—*I'm here, JT.* But JT still couldn't feel Buzz's hand, and he was afraid the voice wasn't Buzz's but the Unicorn feigning Buzz. He was losing himself.

A blue unicorn on a Washington mountainside. If JT reached out to it, it would turn to look at him. So he reached for it. It turned. Then JT remembered only a virgin could touch a unicorn. He pulled his hand back before he could ruin it.

"Don't, you'll scare it away," Roan said to Austin. They were children in bushes, elegant elven eyes blinking amid needled-leaves, hiding like wild animals.

"There is more to this world than heaven and earth," Roan misquoted. JT didn't correct her. JT couldn't remember where they'd been when she said that.

Blood. There was blood. JT could smell it now, and his heart was going like a trip hammer. Blood reflected everywhere in the street puddles of Seattle. JT tried to drop out. It should have been easy. All you did was fall back and out, but there was nowhere to fall back to because the Unicorn was everywhere. —*Buzz? Buzz, get me out of here.* But Buzz didn't answer him, and he felt the glamour blood-scent seep in, setting his orc blood afire. It stoked him with need.

An arrow struck the Unicorn. It sprouted from its neck like disease. A bullet. More. Holes bloomed in the blue. Horse carcasses. Silver-blue horns, bloodstained.

—Buzz, get me out of here!

Swarms of monarch butterflies swirled, unchased.

Roan wept onto Austin's shoulder. JT could taste her tears and grief. "Buzz!" JT didn't know if he was screaming out loud or only in his mind. He could hear nothing but the gunshots and the thrumming of bows. Nothing but horses screaming, Roan's crying, and the whine of a bone saw that sounded like AC fans on high.

Blood wept from the hole in the head of a horse where a unicorn's horn should have been. The mounted policeman didn't seem to notice. "Move along," he said. "Move along." He flipped up his visor, erasing Austin and Roan. It was an old elf JT didn't know.

In a room in Seattle, a bone saw opened Roan's head, and the surgery began.

JT drowned in her tears and the smell of blood. He lashed out at everything, every image, every scent, every sound. He roared like only an orc could roar, loud enough his throat broke and bled.

Buzz found his hand, and the nightmares stopped.

Silence.

Electric gray.

In the gray was a woman, but that was all he could see.

—Who are you? she sent.

JT was afraid of her. Buzz's hand tightened on his.

—I should know you, she sent.

She walked toward him out of nothing. She was a silhouette and watercolor.

—There's something about you. He's tangled up in you. I can almost see him.

She was dark-skinned and lithe as a cattail frond.

—Where's my brother? Where am I?

Her ears stuck out of the halo of her hair, and butterflies circled her.

—Where's Austin?

And JT could see the ghost now.

JT couldn't stand the sight of her. It tore him apart. He fought free, erasing Buzz's touch on his hands, and fell into the real world.

JT hit the ground hard enough to force all the air from his lungs. He'd sprung the door in his need to be away, and fallen two meters to the parking lot pavement and landed flat on his back. Now he couldn't breathe and stars nova-ed in his eyes. Never mind the pain in his back and ribs, he had to be away from here. He scrambled to his feet and ran into the woods.

Behind him people shouted his name. Still in range of the truck, he heard Buzz in his head, —*JT!* He closed the link and ran.

"JT!" he heard behind him. It was Austin. JT ran faster.

"JT." Austin was right behind him now. It didn't matter how fast JT ran, the fucking elf could always outrun him. So he stopped and he spun and he hit him.

He hit him as hard as he could, one good solid crack across the jaw for every goddamn thing Austin had ever done to him: for blindsiding him with that fucking ghost and exposing a wound that JT had never allowed to heal, for all Austin's endless lies, and for forcing JT to leave him when JT had wanted nothing more than to stay. JT hit Austin so hard the elf nearly flew into a backflip. Austin hit the ground. And the elation of seeing Austin laid out flat like that was better than any sex.

Austin didn't move, and for one horrifying, sobering split second, JT thought he'd killed him.

Then Austin groaned, wiped at his jaw, and missed. Now JT was even angrier for having worried one moment about this asshole. Austin tried to push himself up.

"Stay down. Just stay down or I swear by the moon I'll put you back down."

Austin collapsed onto pine needles and dust. He opened his eyes dazedly.

"You know, Austin, the sad thing is that after all the shit you've pulled, I still can't believe you just did that to me. I must be the most naive, gullible, stupidest goddamn orc on the planet. Why didn't you tell me? Why didn't you warn me? Because that was the most . . . the worst . . . Goddamn you. Goddamn you . . ." JT's eyes burned, and the world went blurry. He wiped furiously at them, and his arm came away wet. "Goddamn you. Why?"

"Because if I'd told you what Buzz had found, you wouldn't have believed me."

"Bullshit. You and your fucking bullshit rationalizations—"

"You would never have listened to me. You'd never have helped."

"Bullshit!"

Austin got to his knees and shouted up at him. "It's not bullshit. You know how I know? Because you've done it to me before. Two years ago, you did it to me." JT wanted to shout *bullshit* again and again, but Austin kept on. "After we escaped those wizards and we were holed up in a basement for three weeks hiding, scared, I told you something didn't add up about that job. Something wasn't right. We didn't screw up. It wasn't bad luck. We were sold out. But *you* wouldn't believe me. *You* wouldn't listen to me. And *you* wouldn't help me. *You* left me. You left me alone." Austin punctuated every *you* like everything was JT's fault. Well, it wasn't.

"You were obsessed. You didn't sleep, you didn't eat, you spent hours looking at surveillance tapes with nothing on them. I was not going to stand around and watch you destroy yourself. I begged for you to leave it behind and go with me."

And now it was Austin's eyes that had gone red and watery. "You asked me to forget her!"

"I asked you to give up your crazy conspiracy theory! Sometimes bad things happen. They just happen. And people we love die."

"You see? You see! That's why I had to lie to you: so that I would get the chance to prove I'm not crazy, otherwise you never would have given me one!"

Austin started to get to his feet, and JT bunched up his fists ready to take another swing. "I ain't gonna let you hit me again. Once, I deserved. But that's all you get."

"You didn't let me hit you."

"Please. You ain't a fighter, JT. It doesn't matter that you're strong as a fucking ox. You can't throw a punch worth shit, and you're slow as dirt."

JT let him stand. He might not have been able to throw a punch worth shit, but that swelling jaw was damn satisfying to watch.

Austin pointed back to the truck. "That ghost proves I was right."

"That ghost doesn't prove shit. We don't even know what the fuck it is."

"Buzz knows. You don't want to listen to me? Fine. Listen to Buzz. He'll tell you."

JT looked over at the truck. The words *Country Orc* written down its side looked ridiculous, and JT wished he hadn't painted it there. Buzz and Victor were still in the cab, hidden behind tinted glass.

"If Buzz wasn't in danger, Austin, I would leave you out here, right here in the middle of fucking nowhere. But this isn't over, and Buzz still needs our help. So we're going to do this, and then I'm going home."

Austin started to say something, but JT stopped him. "It doesn't matter, Austin. It doesn't matter whether you're right or you're wrong. That was two years ago. It's ancient history. It ain't bringing Roan or Grayson back. I have a life now. It's a perfectly good life. And once we've finished up this mess, I'm going back to it. So please, just stop it. Stop fucking with me and let me be happy."

JT started back to the truck. Austin didn't follow. "What did she look like, JT?"

Austin sounded so broken that JT almost stopped and went back to him. But that was just Austin's glamour, always calling to JT and adding one more lie. Odysseus lashed to his mast. "It's not her, Austin."

"But what did she look like?"

If they had a pair of VR glasses, Austin could have seen the ghost for himself, but they didn't. Austin, the only person around who actually wanted to see the ghost, couldn't. So thinking it was probably the cruelest thing he could do, JT answered him. "She was wearing a silk dashiki like she used to wear. African patterns. She had butterflies in her hair."

While the boys fought, Buzz and Victor watched from the safety of the truck. Austin was lying flat on the ground with JT standing over him shouting.

Buzz shook his head. "I hate to say it, but I saw that coming. Austin should have just told him the truth from the start. I hope JT ain't mad at me too. I don't think I'd live through a punch like that." He turned to Victor. "Um. Hey. I'm sorry about dragging you into this."

Victor the Wizard shrugged. "This Blue Unicorn, it is priceless."

Buzz turned back to watching the two men outside. "Yeah, I suppose."

"You have a buyer for it already? How much are they going to pay?"

"A buyer? Are you kidding? We ain't selling her. We're going to free her."

They watched the elf and the orc argue.

"I see," Victor the Wizard said.

Finally Austin stood. JT didn't punch him again.

Victor said, "You are right, Buzz. Austin should have told the truth from the start."

CHAPTER NINE

JT checked over his drones, tightening cabling and reloading spent magazines. Everyone was watching him in a long, uncomfortable silence because there was nothing else to do. Except Austin apparently decided every silence was made better by the sound of his voice filling it, so he started to talk. JT almost told him to shut the hell up, but for once Austin was saying something JT wanted to hear.

"Roan found the blue unicorn when we were kids. She wouldn't let me touch it. She said only a virgin could touch a unicorn, and I wasn't a virgin. That was bullshit, because everyone knows blowjobs don't count. But I never did touch it."

Austin took one of the empty curved plastic magazines and began to slot AP rounds into it. It was a make-up gesture. JT wasn't sure if he wanted to make up, but getting any work out of Austin was rare enough, so let the elf load ammo if that's what he wanted.

"A couple years later there was a disease outbreak in our settlement, so Grandfather Henry—he wasn't our grandfather, but he taught us and looked after us, so we called him that—Grandfather Henry led a hunting party . . . and they killed it and took its horn for medicine.

"Roan, she was . . . Well, she didn't understand. She and Grandfather argued, and Roan said she was leaving. She wouldn't study under him anymore, not if magic meant killing something like that. I think it broke Grandfather's heart, her saying that.

"I went with her, not because I thought she was right or Grandfather was wrong, but because I couldn't leave her, so I went with her. We ended up in Seattle. And we . . . we got some money . . . and we found a guy who'd . . . she got the surgery done . . . cortical implants. I always thought . . ."

It wasn't often JT heard Austin stumble when he talked. Had they ever actually talked about Roan after she'd died?

Austin snapped bullets into his magazine, all his attention on it, like there was no one else there. "I always thought she didn't get the implants so she could jack the net. She got them so she couldn't work magic anymore."

JT looked for Victor the Wizard, expecting some response from him. Horror? Disgust? Pity? But Victor wasn't even there. He was just coming out of the dingy restroom and hadn't heard any of it. Probably for the best.

Austin laid his magazine down as JT finished his second. "So there you go: The Blue Unicorn Story."

Back on I-80. This time Buzz rode the middle and Victor was at the passenger window. Austin was in the truck bed lounging amid the recharged, reloaded drones. JT was perfectly fine to have him back there and not in the cab. Outside, endless pine and fir trees blurred past as they drove higher into the Sierra Nevadas. JT kept working his jaw to pop his ears, and he kept ducking his head to look up through the windshield at the sky.

"You nervous?" Buzz said.

"Fuck yeah, I'm nervous. You would be too if you knew what was good for you." He couldn't get as good a look at the sky as he wanted. "Fuck this. Heads-up, Austin," he said through an exterior speaker, and then didn't really give Austin enough time to do anything before the four aerial drones unfolded like metal flowers and took to the air. They dispersed a few hundred meters in cardinal directions, then started a slow orbit around the truck.

JT's mind slipped into three-hundred-sixty-degree vision as if he'd been born to see the world that way. He sighed, relieved, now able to watch everywhere at once. He'd leave the drones out there the rest of the drive to Tahoe; their batteries would last that long at least.

Buzz watched the drones fly off. "Feel better?"

"Maybe. You gonna tell me what happened in there?" JT hadn't meant the question to sound as sharp as it had. Victor made a point of turning farther away from them, a show of offering privacy where there was none.

—*I was there,* Buzz sent through the truck's net.

—*I couldn't feel you there.*

—*It had overloaded your input channels. It took me a moment to realize what it was doing, but once I figured it out—*

—*Why would it do that?*

—*Lashing out at whatever came near it? I don't know. Maybe because it spent the last month imprisoned and poked at by gangsters?*

—*I want to see it again.*

—*That's not safe.*

—*I have to see her again.*

Once it had been Roan always next to him in cyberspace. The way Austin and Grayson had each other's back out in the physical, JT and Roan had been like that too. Early on in their relationship when Bell Anderson had still been coordinating things and they'd flopped in some mansion with an owner gone on holiday, Roan had found JT sprawled out on the couch deep in the net, and she'd asked, "What are you doing?"

Hoping to embarrass her, he said, "Looking at porn."

But of course it didn't. "What kind of porn?"

"My kind of porn."

"You mean guys?"

He opened his eyes and looked at her slyly. "I'm not telling."

"Let me see."

"Uh-uh. You wouldn't like it anyway."

"I like watching guys getting it on with each other."

"Why? They're not interested in you."

"They would be if they met me." Now she was teasing him.

He laughed. "I've met you. I'm still not interested."

"Yeah, well my brother keeps cockblocking me."

JT blushed so furiously it hurt.

"I'm joking, JT."

Well yes, he'd known that, but it made him blush more. "Fine, you wanna look, come on."

She shoved him over to make room for herself on the couch, and he shared the files with her, and they closed their eyes together.

She said, "These are cars."

JT shrugged. He rotated the 3-D images in his head. He flipped through engineering schematics. He reviewed energy transfer efficiency ratios on transmissions. They were all muscle cars, mostly—Corvettes, Chargers, Mustangs—but some exotic performance cars too. He lingered over a 2048 McLaren. It had been Roan's glamour that had gently turned his mind toward the vintage models. What it was about cars, JT never understood. The lines of their bodies, angles, and curves; the way the paint reflected and absorbed the light; the contrast of glass and plastic—JT could never explain to anyone, not even himself, why cars got him hard, but they did. More than once, unthinking, he'd reach out to touch whatever he was looking at, but they were just images and there was nothing to touch.

Roan didn't say anything. JT felt more and more embarrassed, like Roan was watching him jack off.

"Austin teases me about it," he said. "You can too if you want. I don't mind."

"Yes, you do. And Austin's an asshole most of the time."

"Let me show you something." Suddenly excited and confident, he had shown her the design for his truck, the beginning fantasies of the one he drove now. He gave her the grand tour of it, and she asked him to show her its computer, so he created a virtual machine in their shared space.

"May I?" she said when she saw something she thought was off, and he said yes with that hesitant thrill you feel when you finally find someone with whom you can share what you've always wanted to share, but are still terrified they might break it or laugh.

She didn't break it, of course. And she didn't laugh. They worked on his dream side by side for a while, like two friends playing "Heart and Soul" on an old upright piano.

"When someone finally whacks me, I want to come back as a car."

"I don't think it works that way. When I'm whacked, I want to come back as—"

Now what had she said? She hadn't said *unicorn*; she'd said something else. What did it mean that he couldn't remember the important things anymore? Was it just that he hadn't known then to pay attention? Or did it mean that JT had been a shitty friend?

Now it was Buzz next to him in the electric gray nothing. The Blue Unicorn stood in the nondistance. Sometimes the ghost looked like Roan. Sometimes it looked like a pale-blue unicorn with a silver horn. There were always butterflies.

—*Hello*, JT sent to her.

—*Who are you?*

—*Roan? It's JT.* He felt foolish, like a kid playing with a Ouija board.

—*I should know you.*

He shivered, like the same kid when the planchette moved to *yes* and everyone swore it wasn't them that did it. —*It's JT, Roan.*

—*There's something about you.*

It was the same damn thing she'd said before. Some kind of loop. What had he hoped? That she'd be something more? Roan was dead.

To Buzz he sent, —*Forget the glamour for now, what is it?*

—*I told you, an AI fragment.*

—*Roan wasn't an AI.*

—*No, but somewhere there's an AI that was created using Roan's memories as seeds.*

—*You're saying that someone stole her memories to make an AI? Someone stole her glamour? How is that even possible?* The idea of it made him feel vaguely ill. Stealing Roan's glamour seemed too much like stealing her soul.

—*No one stole anything.* She *built this. Roan figured out how to code a glamour.*

—*Roan didn't do AI research.*

—*Apparently she did. Her style is all over this code.*

—*You can fake coding style.*

—*I can, yes. But it's not easy, JT. Authorship identification heuristics look for things you don't think to fake: frequency of comments, how data type declarations are organized, frequency of capital letters in variable names, even line spacing. It's the same kind of Bayesian analysis lit historians use to tell whether it was Octavia Butler or N.K. Jemisin who wrote some unsigned story. Roan's style is all over this thing. And if you don't believe that, then believe her glamour. Because you know that's her glamour, JT.*

Old thoughts arose, old scents, half-forgotten. Melancholy, that's what the Blue Unicorn's glamour was. That was Roan's glamour: melancholy. Not like Austin's glamour at all, all war-lust and fucking. Was that why JT had remembered that time he'd confessed his car fetish and she hadn't laughed at him?

And other things JT remembered now: plastic trays on recycled plastic tables, no ham in the macaroni and cheese. Didn't they know that orcs needed meat? Older orc kids spooning food for younger orcs, tusks not come in yet. Melancholy like the rows of adult orcs that had filed by, all in identical laboratory clothes, and nameless JT-1138 (they were all nameless then, only letters and numbers) had stopped eating. All of them stopped eating or talking, forks half raised, and turned to watch the adults in their line, wondering which of them might be Ma or Da, because just one single glance from any of those adults—any acknowledgment at all—would mean something to a six-year-old born and raised in a lab. But the adults wouldn't look at them, not for nothing.

JT shook it off. It was Roan's glamour. He couldn't deny it.

Buzz sent, —*Somewhere out there is an AI that Roan created out of her own memories and glamour. Hiding maybe. But two years ago, someone found out it existed, so they set you all up, and they killed her for it. That's what me and Austin think.*

—*Fuck what Austin thinks.*

—*What about me, then? Fuck what Buzz thinks too? It may be hypothetical, but it's not crazy, JT. Look at what the Electric Dragon has thrown at us, and that was just to recover that ghost. Imagine what they would do to actually get hold of an AI with a glamour?*

The Blue Unicorn flickered between its forms. —*Who is it you're talking to? Is that Austin?*

—*No, it's Buzz.* Damn Austin. And now Buzz had caught Austin's crazy too. JT was the only one left sane enough to see how much bullshit it all was. There was no fucking conspiracy, just one big fucking mistake.

—*This entity Buzz does not fit your edges. Austin belongs there. Austin is what fits. That is how I know you. You are Austin's edges.*

If it kept asking for Austin, then fine, he'd give her Austin. —*Austin's here.*

—*What are you doing?* Buzz sent. —*JT, I don't think that's a good idea.*

JT didn't care. He flipped a camera so that half of the gray nothing became an image of the truck bed. Austin lay there dozing.

—*Austin?* The Blue Unicorn's sending felt odd. The timbre was off. It echoed through the tiny cyberspace of the truck.

—*It's pushing at ports,* Buzz sent. —*I'm closing them. You shouldn't have done that.*

—*Austin!* the Blue Unicorn sent.

JT activated security protocols. —*Shut her down, Buzz.*

—*I'm working on it. Goddamn it, you shouldn't have done that!*

—*Austin!* The wave of data slammed into him. Blue static. Blue lightning. Butterflies sparking digital. JT closed ports and shut down processes, anything he could do to stop her attack without stopping the truck and drones cold. It wasn't enough.

—*She's transmitting.*

—*Transmitting what?*

—*Our location.*

—*Shut everything down. Everything!* Suddenly JT couldn't see. Suddenly he was shoved back into himself, eyes blinking, heart pounding, and he had no control over anything, not anything. The truck skewed, no longer following the road. He reached out to the system. It was dead. The tires growled on the gravel curb. The truck bounced crazily and caught air and dipped toward an embankment. Victor shouted. Pine trees rushed them at two hundred kilometers per hour.

And JT was back in. Just as fast as he'd been kicked out, he was back in and the truck's wheels and the truck's transmission were part of him again. They might as well have been his feet or his legs. He slowed and skipped over broken stones and pine needles and angled his way back toward the road. He didn't slide on the gravel shoulder or fishtail. Smooth asphalt back under him, JT reconnected with a GPSat and refigured his course.

He opened his eyes and remembered to breathe. See? Nothing to it.

Buzz and Victor were staring at him wide-eyed. Austin was still deep in his elf-sleep in the truck bed.

"Should have warned you," JT said.

"You think?"

"Did her transmission go through?"

"Did you crash your truck and kill us all? I'm not incompetent."

"I said I'm sorry."

"No, actually, you didn't."

"Sorry."

Buzz shook his head. "I'm starting to understand Austin a lot more."

"Do you know who she was contacting?"

Buzz shook his head. "All nodes multicast," meaning the Blue Unicorn was just trying to blast their location every-damn-where.

And for whatever reason, it had been the sight of Austin that had triggered it.

JT's 360° panorama view: Lake Tahoe was its uncanny blue again. The druids had done that. On the other side of the blue: mountains. Pine and fir everywhere. There was a strong wind. White caps on the lake, white caps on mountaintops.

Through a camera looking back into the truck bed, he saw Austin staring off into the forest and the glimpses of a lake through the trees. Austin was talking to himself and waving his hand slowly like he was working out some muscle kink. The wind staticked up the microphone back there, and JT could barely pick out Austin's words. "Down to two. If you think . . . go ahead go . . . where . . . meet us? Yeah, yeah, . . . can't get lost."

"Who are you talking to?" JT said through a speaker.

"You know that's fucking rude, right?" Austin said to the air.

JT sulked and left him alone.

The entrance to the Crossed Pines Resort was marked by a small shack and a sign. JT slowed, but there was no one there in the shack. He kept on going. "Fuck, where are they?"

"They won't come till I give the signal," Buzz said.

"Not 3djinn. The Electric Dragon."

"JT, I've been planting a lot of bad data as we've been going. There ain't a cop or a government agent in Pacifica who could find us unless they actually saw us drive by. The Electric Dragon ain't gonna find us either. We've made it."

"We haven't made it. Where the fuck are they?"

They drove another five K down a single-lane road that twisted through pine trees. Tucked amid the woods, the resort's lodge house stood some thirty meters up a shallow incline from the lake's rocky beach. It was a three-story log home layered with broad, terraced porches and blocked with large dark windows. Behind the house on top of a small, rocky outcropping partly hidden behind trees stood a circle of standing stones with a sacrificial altar slab in their center. A path connected the outcropping to the lodge house.

There were no other cars in the gravel lot—no people, no one down on the beach, and no one at the wide dock or its small fleet of sailboats. One kilometer out, JT's eyes-in-the-air tracked only crows, probably the druids' eyes watching them. No sign of any other people for kilometers around. The place looked mothballed even in June.

JT parked the truck in the lodge house's gravel lot. Buzz disconnected the Blue Unicorn's crystal data block and tucked it in his overshirt pocket, and they all piled out to the ground.

There was something eerie about this place, and it wasn't just invisible druids. There was a quiet here that JT had felt only once or twice in his life, but he couldn't place what was missing. Bird whistles, insect chirps, the splash of fish, those were all there. "There's no network here," he finally realized. Nearly everywhere in the world, JT heard the background hiss of the net, the hum of electricity in wires, or the sleek clicking of optical cables and switches. Here, there was barely any of that. There were no wireless towers.

"Nope," Buzz said with a proud little smirk. "The only perfect security for a paranoid hacker is a place with no net. And the druids keep it that way."

Buzz walked down the sidewalk that led past the enormous wooden deck of the lodge and stood near the docks. The wind tossed his hair around and tangled his overshirt around his waist. He had his hands buried in his pockets and was looking out over the water. Sailboats tethered to the dock swayed behind him and knocked against foam bumpers. Anyone would look dramatic and heroic standing with a backdrop like that. The sun burned Buzz's hair rich copper, and the sight of it struck a chord in JT, deep and old like Roan's glamour had touched him.

JT caught up to Buzz. "You shouldn't be by yourself." They walked together out onto the dock. JT's clunky work boots thudded on the wooden planking. Water lapped at the dock's pylons, and sailboats creaked. The air smelled of pine and water, cleaner than anything JT had ever smelled, even in the desert. "So where they gonna take you?"

Buzz shrugged. "Dunno. High Castle, probably." He didn't sound enthused.

High Castle was 3djinn's net. JT hadn't known it was also a real place. On impulse, he said, "You could come with me."

"With you?"

"Back to Greentown. You'll like it. It's quiet there."

"Quiet?" Buzz said like he didn't know what the word meant.

"You need a place to hide out for a while. I'm just saying: my place is open. Or you could get an apartment if you decided to stay."

Buzz gave him a funny look, like he was trying to figure JT out but couldn't. "Thanks." It wasn't a yes.

Buzz took a small spray can out of his pocket and shook it. A mixing ball rattled inside it. "UV paint. Nontoxic, water soluble, druid approved." He knelt on the dock and started painting what might have been the 3djinn logo of three crossed scimitars but turned out more like a wobbly asterisk. Or that's the way it would have looked if the paint had been visible.

"What? So they shine a black light on it?"

Buzz pointed up to the sky. "Crows. Crows can see into the UV."

"The druids are allied with 3djinn?"

"'Ally' is a strong word."

One of the crows flying overhead changed course and flew south over the water. And who knew whether that had anything to do with the symbol Buzz had painted or whether it was just random bird behavior. That was probably the point.

They headed back for the truck. Austin was coming down the path to meet them. He had his bow and a handful of arrows in one hand and was striking a rock across their tips to transfer the rock's power to the broadheads, charging them for his magic.

"You feel it too," JT said.

Austin joined them. "Oh yeah. Something's coming."

Buzz looked around, but there wasn't anything to see. "You got some elf sixth sense going?"

"Yeah, it's called experience."

"Guys, we made it," Buzz said. "3djinn's—"

Austin shushed him. He cocked his head like he heard something. He looked at JT. JT shook his head no, he saw nothing 360°.

They stood there, unmoving. Buzz tried to say something, but JT hissed him quiet again. A fish splashed beneath the dock.

Austin looked off into the trees to the west. He smiled an evil smile. "Really? You're going to fight an elf in the woods? Well, that's just goddamn stupid." He glanced back to JT. "They're coming in on foot."

And finally JT saw them in the air. "And two Nightshrikes."

The three of them sprinted up the walk toward JT's truck.

"Keep her safe," Austin said to JT, and with a glance to Buzz added, "Him too, I guess." Then he veered off toward the woods, whispering spells, bow in one hand, six arrows in the other. A moment later, he was hidden from view behind trees, and JT slid to a stop across gravel, one arm out to stop Buzz too.

Near JT's truck, Victor glided around like he was ballroom dancing or something, but what he was doing was tracing patterns in the gravel with his foot. There were circles and sigils drawn everywhere, and JT had stopped just short of crossing one of Victor's lines.

Victor the Wizard saw them and froze in place with one foot extended, bathrobe and pajama pants flapping in the wind, and gave JT a crazy look, and it wasn't just the mismatched eyes. "I'm sorry, JT. It's nothing personal. But you have shitty taste in friends." He glared at Buzz. "You betrayed me. It's your fault my apartment was destroyed and my life ruined. And Austin shouldn't have lied."

JT dove for one of the sigils, hoping to break it, but Victor swept his foot and closed off his last diagram, and JT was too late. Sheets of yellow light flashed and rocketed around the air. The wind went wild. Lights strobed across the elaborate pattern as if they were bullets ricocheting off invisible walls.

Buzz ducked. JT scrambled away from the lights, not wanting to know what would happen if one of them touched him.

Victor shook his fists in the air. "You shouldn't have lied to Victor the Transmuter!" Then the lights all vanished into the truck as if it were a black hole sucking in everything. Profound silence, not even birds.

And, just for a moment, JT thought Victor's spell hadn't worked. "What was that supposed to—"

Pop!—like a balloon bursting. Pain lanced through JT's head, and his vision suddenly contracted to what he could see with his own two spot-filled eyes. He lost contact with his airborne drones. He lost contact with the truck. In a split second of pure panic, he rattled through a dozen protocols to access his truck, but none of them got any response. The truck was utterly dead and his communications hub with it. The airborne drones were out of range, as dead as his truck. "What have you done?"

"I turned all the gold in your truck into lead," Victor the Transmuter said. "It never hurts to know a little science."

JT roared. "You broke my truck!" His vision tunneled down to one scrawny wizard in a godsdamned bathrobe, and he charged. He would tear the fucker limb from limb. He would eat the wizard's fucking heart while it was still fucking beating. He would—

A hand wave from Victor and the ground fell out from beneath JT. JT dropped jaw-snappingly hard into a pit that hadn't been there a moment before, stunned senseless.

CHAPTER TEN

These woods were magical. Austin felt the trees close around him. The presence he'd sensed in the woods darkened and grew. He'd felt that presence before. It was Owen Ren Leng, the necromancer, back from the dead. Again.

A wizard's power came from words and symbols. Austin's power came from the same place as a druid's. It was why he went barefoot: in lands like these, where druids ruled, he could pull power from the unabused earth. It was why he carried certain rocks: sometimes the land had gone too long abused and he needed a purer source. Sometimes you needed both. He pulled out the rock JT had found for him and whispered to it. He curled his toes around cool pine needles. He bound the shadows of the needles and the mottling of bark to himself. A magical camouflage flickered over him. He felt silken, like light itself could not touch him. Crumbled stone sifted through his fingers to the ground.

Out there, through pine trees noble and green guarding ochre land, 49ers moved, heard, not seen. Not one of them had a ghost of a chance.

"Give it to me, Buzz," Victor said.

Buzz backed away. He knew he should run, but he was scared shitless and could barely move. "You shouldn't be doing this, Vic." He put his hand over his pocket where the data block was. "Why are you doing this?"

Victor advanced, evil-wizard style, and did that thing he did with the violet plasma arcing from hand to hand that had always seemed so cool before. Not so much now. "They'll forgive me for helping you, if I help them. Give me the Unicorn, Buzz!"

Buzz shook his head no, but his hand plucked at his pocket like some better-sensed part of him knew when to give up. Then he saw JT crawling out of the shallow pit Victor had clobbered him with, and JT's eyes were red as laser lights, and his tusks flashed like they were made of steel. JT was pissed off as fuck, far scarier than anything Victor could pull off, crazy eyes and plasma or not.

JT was going to save him.

Someday it would be Buzz saving someone. Someday it would be Buzz who made someone else feel the way JT made Buzz feel now. Buzz broke out in a crazy smile, all the warning Victor needed.

Drone One had survived San Francisco. It was in the back of the truck, close enough JT didn't need his truck's amplifier to control it. For all the hate and rage and pain pumping through him, JT wasn't mindless, he wasn't an animal. And Drone One could see just fine. JT unloaded with Drone One right into the wizard's back.

Bullets into snowballs, same trick as before, but JT didn't care. JT unloaded. JT knew what it was like to be hit by a supersonic snowball. *Take a hundred, you traitorous fuck.*

Victor flew three meters from all the snow that hit him.

JT stopped firing.

One of Victor's arms stuck out of the pile of snow, limp and unmoving.

JT huffed on the edge of the pit. He looked at Buzz cowering, all that beautiful fear on his face. Lust and a vague thought to take Buzz sparked through JT. He had defeated the wizard and now here was his prize. Take him. *Take him,* some part of him said. The idea so instinctive and compelling it was almost enough to distract him from what really mattered. Almost.

"My truck," JT whined. "My goddess-blessed truck." It looked no different than before, but all the truck's conductive surfaces and the nano-engineered gold catalyst in his fuel cells were gone, turned to lead, and the truck was useless now.

"JT." Buzz tried to pull JT away from his broken truck. JT batted the little guy away. JT wasn't entirely sure even he could fix it. He'd have to gut the whole thing. Every single electrical component in the whole blessed thing. Victor should have just killed JT. It couldn't have hurt any worse than seeing his truck like this.

"JT, they're coming."

It would feel so good to pop that fucking wizard right in the head. Let's see how he likes it. He pulled the pistol from the belt of his jeans, smart system autoconnecting, and flipped the safety off.

"JT, the 'copters!"

Something struck his arm, a lame punch from Buzz to get his attention, just as a lashing wind storm kicked up: two Nightshrikes coming over the tree line. That snapped him out of it.

JT grabbed Buzz by the collar and dragged him along as if it had been his idea to run. One Nightshrike opened fire just as they ducked beneath the wooden deck. Wood cracked and splintered. JT and Buzz wove through supports and braces, trying to get as close to the foundation wall of the lodge as they could, so as to put as much deck between them and the bullets as possible, but even down here the air was filled with splinters.

The gunfire stopped as the second Nightshrike landed and disgorged soldiers to follow them. They were kitted out like the ones in San Francisco had been: body armor, smart helmets, QCW-10 submachine guns, and runeblades.

JT and Buzz circled to the downhill side of the lodge and onto yet another deck, one floor lower than the last and overlooking the lake. There were bench seats and fire pits built into it. A full wall of glass sliding doors opened into the lodge. The doors were unlocked. JT and Buzz ducked inside and slid the door closed behind them.

"What are we gonna do?" Buzz panicked as they crawled fast through the lounge they had found. Couches and half walls broke up the space, hiding them from anyone looking in from the deck. Halls led off to conference rooms, glass-walled and covered with vertical blinds for privacy. Outside, they heard bootfalls on the decking. They chose a hallway at random and fled down it. "We're fucked, JT."

"We ain't fucked. We got Drone One. Now all we need is a Nightshrike."

Five of the Electric Dragon's 49ers lay dead, and that's when Austin felt the cold. Tahoe in June was never hot, but this was cold, real cold. It seeped straight to the bone, and a mist that wasn't there moments ago stirred around his feet.

He pressed against a tree, camouflage hiding him perfectly. He listened. The whine of Nightshrike rotors was dull in the trees. The gunfire back toward the lodge had stopped. That meant JT and Buzz had gone to ground somewhere; they were safe. Or it meant they were dead. JT was two years out of practice, and he'd never been caught in the thick of things anyway. Christ, had Austin just gotten his best friend killed?

No. JT is pro. JT is top bill. JT is fine. Do your job. Listen. The necromancer is here.

An icy breeze came from the other side of the tree. Austin inched his way around it. Bark tugged at the back of his nylon combat jacket.

A man in Chinese robes and jade floated a meter off the ground in the center of a small clearing. He carried his staff of bone capped by a skeletal hand. The hand twitched and its fingers curled and uncurled.

"I can smell you, Austin Shea," said the Necromancer Owen Ren Leng. His voice was like fingernail scratches on rough paper. The necromancer touched his staff to one of Austin's victims lying dead on the ground. The corpse twitched and struggled to stand. "Do you see the irony, here? Strike my soldiers down—you only make my army more powerful."

Yeah, Austin had caught that. Well, they'd smashed him into a cloud of joss paper before, hadn't they? They could do it again. All Austin needed was a big-ass truck to run him over with.

The necromancer turned in a slow circle, staff in front of him. Owen Ren Leng might have been able to smell Austin, but he still didn't know where Austin was, and Austin had no intention of giving himself away until he had a plan. It grew colder. Austin's breath misted.

He didn't know if his camouflage extended to his breath. He breathed as shallowly and slowly as he could.

The dead soldier got his feet under him and swayed. Austin's other victims emerged from the darkening woods. Zombies with submachine guns. Just fucking great. Austin stayed still as a mouse, hoping to God his camouflage held against whatever senses the undead had.

Joss paper everywhere, Austin thought again. Yes, carefully folded and tucked beneath cloth and jade, the necromancer's hands and fingers were made of paper. His neck was made of paper. Owen Ren Leng wasn't human at all. He was a ghost inhabiting a body made from hell money.

Hell money was meant to be burned.

Austin nocked an arrow and swung out from hiding. He loosed a rope of orange flame. Without looking, he knew he hit. Austin always hit. He ran, circling wide. Second arrow: rope of flame. They might not have been able to see him, but they could see the flame every time he shot. Gunfire incoming. Roll. Rattle of submachine guns. Bark flew and the air went thick with pine scent. Third arrow, fire-blossom, zombie gunfire behind him. Keep moving, keep moving. Fourth arrow, his last. Behind a tree, he caught his breath and dared to look.

Three thin streams of fire ran the paths Austin's arrows had flown. They crossed like a burning asterisk or the beginnings of a spider's web or 3djinn's logo. Pinned, run-through three times in the asterisk's center was the Necromancer Owen Ren Leng. The fourth arrow burned, caught in the hand of the necromancer's staff, the Withered Arm of some Chinese Hell King. Austin counted that as a hit. The necromancer's elaborate robes began to smolder. Small fires caught all over him. The necromancer hissed and writhed like a snake, but that didn't set him free; all it did was start more little fires as the flaming ropes twisted around him.

Then the necromancer breathed icy breath on the arrow grasped in the staff's skeletal hand. The arrow frosted over. Its fire guttered and died. There was a crackle in the air and the fog became thicker. The fiery ropes flickered and went out. The patches of flame on his robes and where paper had caught faltered and died.

Frost swirled out from Owen Ren Leng and glazed the ground. It ran in lacy patterns everywhere and swept beneath Austin's feet. Austin had walked barefoot nearly all his life—cold concrete, snow, ice, he was used to—but this frost was nothing like that. This frost struck him numb. He leapt away. It didn't matter whether the necromancer could see him; the frost was thickening, the cold was everywhere. He had to get out of here.

He needed more power; more than he could draw from the land or a stone. Enough power to create a conflagration Owen Ren Leng couldn't extinguish with his deathly cold. And Austin knew just where to get it.

"A Nightshrike?" Buzz said. "JT, I'm never going to be able to hack that system. Not on the fly like this. It's military-grade encryption, and I don't have a back door."

They were hunkered beneath a conference table in one of the glass rooms, whispering. Their entry into the room had stirred up enough breeze to make the vertical blinds sway. JT watched them, wishing they'd stop.

"Right," JT said. "So we need a direct patch into their system. And you're not going to do it; I am."

"How are you going to do that?"

"Grab one of those soldiers."

"By yourself? Are you nuts?"

"I ain't risking you."

"Very fucking noble. By which I mean stupid. You'll have to keep him conscious and you'll have about a tenth of a second to take over his system and shut him out of his own hardware. He ain't going to just stand there while you do that."

And of course Buzz was right, but that wasn't the point. And he was going to explain that, but Buzz put one hand on JT's shoulder. It felt good there. "I helped you before, didn't I?" Buzz said.

"Yeah, but—" JT thought of blue fire. He thought of how he'd frozen seeing Buzz go into his trance back at the apartment. And this plan here, this was a whole hell of a lot more dangerous than hacking the Bay Area Traffic Net.

"I'm not a kid, JT. I told you, I'm done with working in the background. I can do this, and you . . . it's not really your thing. I mean you're not terrible, not with out-of-box configurations, but—"

JT shushed him. The hallway went darker. Someone had moved into it and was blocking the light filtering in from outside. The blinds had almost stopped swaying. But the soldiers would be moving in pairs at the very least, low-light, UV, and IR vision all slaved to their smart-guns. There was no way to hide from them, blinds swaying or still. And, heavy as it looked, this table they were under would probably only stop the first few bullets before it all blew into splinters.

"Fine," JT said. He gave Buzz a quick kiss so awkward one tusk nicked Buzz's ear. Buzz was 3djinn, he told himself. Buzz was every bit as good as Roan had been. (But Roan had died. No, don't think about that.)

JT had maneuvered Drone One inside through a side door on the floor above them. It was a minute away, but that was a guess. He brought it down a staircase, clumsy as hell. Next drone he built would have six legs, not four.

Shadows grew and faded as the soldiers in the hall went door to door. Across the lodge, Drone One descended step by step. Buzz produced a patch cable from one of the pockets of his shorts. He flipped aside hair and plugged the cable into a skull jack. He worried the other end in his hand. They stayed crouched beneath the conference table, wheeled chairs around them.

Drone One made the bottom of the stairs. JT moved it down the hall, not quite sure how to get through the maze of shaded rooms to the one where they were hiding. Drone One wasn't subtle at all. Its legs clunked on the rug-strewn floors, and it was going to draw attention before JT wanted it to.

Buzz was sweating, anxiety like the bouquet of a wine. JT blew the scent out from his nose. He checked his smart pistol, marked Buzz as friendly.

Shadows at the door. The handle turned.

Somewhere in the lodge, a pair of Electric Dragon soldiers rounded a corner and saw Drone One.

"Shit," JT said. The soldiers opened fire on the drone. Bullets pinged off nano-engineered steel and ceramic plating and the glass walls all around it shattered from reflected shots.

The handle stopped turning. The soldiers outside the door were going to run toward the gunfire and join the rest of their squad. It would ruin everything.

JT dropped the pistol, hefted the entire table, and ran it like a mahogany battering ram. He plowed straight through the door and shattered the wall. Aluminum framing folded like cardboard. Two 49ers folded like cardboard. JT tripped on debris and hurled the table through the far wall of the hall even as he crashed to the glass-strewn floor, right alongside one of the soldiers. The soldier swung his QCW-10 around, and JT wrenched it out of his hand and flung it down the hallway. The soldier tried to draw his sword. JT pounced, swinging wild and hard as he could. The soldier's helmet absorbed everything, so JT tore the helmet off, ripping though nylon and snapping plastic. Beneath it was a young man, nose bloodied.

Buzz shouted, "Fuck! The gun ain't working! JT!"

The second 49er flung the table off her and brought up her QCW-10. JT leapt away, but there wasn't a bit of ground not covered in some broken thing, and JT stumbled again. He tangled in the cords of a set of blinds, and pulled the whole damn thing down on top of him when he fell. Bullets tore through the space he'd been in.

The soldier cast her gun aside and pulled her sword. It burst into flame, and its edges went red, then orange hot.

Buzz cussed up a storm and tried to fire JT's gun again, but it was slaved to JT and wouldn't do what Buzz wanted. JT fired it for him. Buzz yelped and dropped it, surprised. The helmetless soldier had been in a bad spot and fell dead with two holes in his head.

A flaming sword swept too near Buzz's throat. Buzz squealed and tried to fall back, but the soldier grabbed Buzz by the neck with one hand and lifted him off the ground as if he weighed nothing at all. Buzz's face went instantly purple, and he made a horrible noise. The soldier hauled her sword back to gut him.

JT dropped a loop of cord around the soldier's neck and pulled tight as he fucking could. The soldier dropped both Buzz and her sword and clawed at the cord on her throat. She clawed at JT.

The soldier's right arm was mechanical and strong as fuck. It clamped down around JT's wrist and would have snapped it clean if the angle had been better. JT yanked the cord harder. "Buzz," JT hissed, gritting his teeth. The mechanical hand closed tighter. It would crush his wrist. "Buzz!"

No one being strangled thought about network security. They thought about getting air and getting free. Buzz snapped his patch cable into the soldier's helmet jack.

"Her arm," JT said, "Shut down her fucking arm!"

Buzz did more than that. The soldier dropped unconscious in JT's arms. The hand on JT's wrist relaxed.

"Got her," Buzz said, happily, hoarsely, eyes slightly unfocused. Then his eyes went wide and very focused. "Oh shit. They've got—" and Buzz collapsed to the floor.

Austin sprinted, threading trees. Owen Ren Leng followed, sailing airborne. His gold-and-red robes billowed behind him. Austin was certain the necromancer couldn't see him, but either the heat of Austin's body or simply the fact that Austin was alive called the necromancer to him, sight or no sight.

Frost chased Austin. It glazed trees and turned the soft carpet of pine needles into knives. Austin would have left bloody footprints behind him if he weren't constantly calling on the land to cover his passing. Had he finished his own studies as a druid instead of following a more violent path, maybe the spirit of this place would have accepted his blood as a sacrifice. He prayed that the unknown spirit might anyway. One never knew.

Zombies chased also. These weren't the slow kind of zombies Owen Ren Leng had created before. These ran on all fours, howling like they were possessed by hounds, trailing their own blood and gore behind them. The necromancer whirled his Withered Arm over his head, spurring them ever faster.

Austin burst from the woods out onto the gravel lot. Overhead, two Nightshrikes swung around the lodge house. A squad of Electric Dragon soldiers sprinted low across one of the lodge's many decks.

That meant JT was still alive and kicking ass. Austin raced toward the soldiers faster than anything other than a fox had a right to go. His camouflage flickered gray gravel, trees, and sky as he ran. Undead chased after him.

Austin drew one final draft of power from the land, and he leapt four meters onto the lodge deck and plowed right through the line of soldiers. The zombie hounds dug unnatural claws into wood and hurtled themselves after him. The soldiers panicked at the sight of their dead brethren transformed, mauled, and eyes glowing green, and they opened fire on them, chewing through ballistic cloth and reanimated flesh. The zombies fell on them, enraged and uncaring who they slaughtered. Owen Ren Leng swept up and over them all, fighting for control over the butchery beneath him. And Austin slipped past it all, unseen.

"Buzz!" JT shouted. His blood went cold and his stomach knotted and he couldn't breathe right. He couldn't move. He could only stare down at Buzz sprawled out on the floor. *No,* he told himself. *No, he's not dead. He's okay. It's a hacker's trance, is all. There's no smoke, no reddening of the skin from internal burns, none of that awful smell of burnt hair and burnt electronics. None of that. He's okay. He'll be okay as long as I don't stand here like an idiot.*

He dropped the soldier in his arms and knelt by Buzz. Buzz whispered words too fast and too quiet to follow. Beneath closed lids, his eyes darted like he was in REM sleep. JT felt his pulse at his neck. It was racing, but not dangerously so. The Electric Dragon had brought a network specialist of their own, and Buzz was deep in the Nightshrike's cyberspace fighting for his life. JT grabbed the patch cord, thumb on the tab that held it in place. He almost pulled it. Probably, he should have pulled it. Instead he let go.

He tore the helmet off the unconscious soldier and fit it over Buzz's head and fastened the chin strap. He tucked the excess patch cord down Buzz's T-shirt so it wouldn't tangle or catch. And he hefted Buzz over his shoulder like he was a buck sixty of nothing. All JT had to do was keep Buzz safe and let Buzz do the rest.

Down the hall, grenade canisters clacked against a wall and spewed thick gas. JT ran down the hall, away from the gas, knowing that was exactly what they wanted him to do.

The druid's circle was a modern one, its granite stones precision cut by a water saw, one by three by nine. The circle was open on the quarter that faced the lodge. The rest of it was covered by a series of lintel stones. It seemed like poor placement for a circle, Austin thought, since trees would block out the star lines, but the sloping altar stone in the center had been well-used. In the forty-odd years since the Awakening, sacrifices had left the altar streaked with dark stains. He hoped these druids were Reformed and not Boudican Adventists. The thought that the power he was about to draw upon might have come from ritually murdered people made Austin queasy.

He struck an arrow against the altar, expecting sparks and flash of heat as the power transferred. He got nothing at all.

That didn't seem likely, so he tried it again and got nothing again. He swore.

And then he saw the markings. They were small and had been scratched with a nail or a sharp rock's edge. They weren't Celtic runes. They were nothing a druid would use. They were wizard's symbols, Hermetic tradition. Not Owen Ren Leng. Victor. Victor had already claimed the power here. Austin had almost forgotten about the wizard entirely. Victor would be with JT and Buzz, all the power of a druid's circle at the wizard's disposal.

Austin smiled, imagining the look on Owen Ren Leng's nonexistent face when Victor unloaded. Down below him all hell finally broke loose. He sprinted down the path, feeling terribly smug in his decision to bring the wizard along, and afraid he would miss the whole glorious thing.

They were herding JT with tear gas back outside. There would be soldiers waiting for him there. Drone One was his only chance.

The pneumatics on one of Drone One's legs was shot to hell, and it lurched as JT ran it through hallways to join him. They burst back into the lounge that opened out onto the lakeside deck at the same time: Drone One from the hallway in one corner; JT from another.

The wall of glass doors shattered—all of it—and through it came a raving horde of . . . what? People, once, but what were they now? Not zombies, but something even more feral, crazed, and ruined. And goddamn they were fast.

He unloaded with Drone One, but all that did was push them back a bit. He kept firing and firing. He swept the drone's guns across the swarm of fiends, back and forth. Gore splattered everywhere and still, impossibly, they inched forward, pushing against the hailstorm of bullets like they were walking into a wind.

JT turned to run back. Even tear gas was better than this. But through the gas he saw the flames of blurred runeswords advancing, soldiers wearing gas masks. He was trapped. Outside, a Nightshrike descended to the deck, its rotors loud as a freight train.

"Please tell me that's yours," JT said to Buzz, still cradled in his arms and deep in his hacker's trance.

It wasn't Buzz's. The Nightshrike opened fire with its forward-mounted machine gun. Its large-caliber bullets smashed Drone One to scrap.

Then the Nightshrike's glass cockpit went white with spider-web cracks and burst. The Nightshrike spun crazy, yawing upward and back as if it were being sucked away. Its rotors clipped the deck and snapped, and the whole thing spun out into the lake.

A second Nightshrike took its place.

In all the din, Buzz's voice was almost too quiet. "Duck."

JT dropped to the floor, and the air filled with bullets and zombie gore. JT drew tight over Buzz's body and glass and plaster and blood and bone and other things JT even didn't want to know rained down on him. The noise of it was deafening. The silence when it was over even more.

Dust settled.

Buzz opened his big brown eyes. "You're really heavy."

JT shifted. "Sorry."

"Did we win?"

Here's a half-formed tableau: JT and Buzz in a Greentown pizzeria. JT would talk about his work. Buzz would talk about his. They would laugh and have a beer or two and maybe they'd kiss over the table or hold hands under it. He supposed it was a date he was almost dreaming of, the kind of everyday date you had with everyday guys: nice, quiet guys. Buzz wasn't everyday anymore, was he? And he was never going to give up the thrill of what he'd just done. Not for pizza. So JT smiled, but only a little. "Yeah. Yeah, we won."

"So kiss me, then."

But before JT could decide what to do, Victor said, "How romantic," and dropped the ceiling on them both.

There was so much dust and debris in the air, Austin couldn't see a thing. He coughed and tried to breathe through a sleeve. He tried drawing power for a spell, but he was on wooden decking and not touching ground. As he had raced down the path toward the lodge, he'd seen one Nightshrike open fire on the other, then half the lodge had caved in. He shouted through the dust, "JT? Victor?" And through the dust he saw a form. He nocked an arrow, unable to tell who it was.

"Austin?" It was Victor.

Austin called back, "What happened? Where's—" and a breeze kicked up and swept the dust away, and there was Victor the Wizard framed by the gaping wound in the side of the lodge that had once been its lakeside facing. Victor's left eye was dark as a lunar eclipse; his right blazed like the heart of a sun with stolen druidic power. And suspended in the air to either side of Victor, limp as stringless puppets, hung JT and Buzz. Only endless optimism told Austin they were still alive.

And the way Victor stood there—his smug look and his lack of care for the two unconscious men he held in the air—Austin finally figured it out: Victor had betrayed them.

"Come out where I can see you, Austin."

And for one split second Austin was confused. He was standing right there in broad daylight, a deer in headlights. Victor should have killed him ten times over by now. Austin had forgotten his camouflage: his body flickered with the blue of the lake and the sky, white/gray striated wood planking, and Victor couldn't see Austin at all.

Owen Ren Leng rounded the corner of the lodge. "I see you. Your life is like a pestilence to me. Surrender. Lay down your bow. You have no magic left. Your arrows are useless. The fight is done."

"It ain't done till I'm dead." He shifted his aim from one wizard to the other, knowing the necromancer was right and one arrow wasn't enough.

"Lay down your bow, and you can have your friend."

"No, he can't!" Victor said. "Buzz and the ghost are yours, JT and Austin are mine, that was the agreement." He cackled and called out to the air as if Austin were some wind spirit, "Do you have any idea the bounty on your head, Austin? All those years pissing on every crime lord and corporation on the West Coast has left you with few friends." He glanced at JT. "Even your partner doesn't want you around."

JT was bloody and battered to hell. His ruined clothes were caked with layers of filth. And all that was covered in white dust from the collapse. It was Austin's fault JT had left him. And now it was Austin's fault JT had been hurt. Austin ground his teeth. Victor the Wizard's one eye seemed to brighten with madness, all that power bound up in one silver orb.

"Nebraska, get me that rock, boy. Fetch me that rock."

Austin's familiar streaked in like a golden-furred comet. His claws skittered rapid-fire on the deck, scraped as he slid around corners. Then Nebraska leapt, and with his tiny claws and teeth tore the argent-fired Eye of Horus from Victor's eye socket and, quick as a blink, dropped it into Austin's open hand.

Austin struck the broadhead against it like striking a match. It flared white and then orange as Austin let fly. The arrow cut the binding thread of Owen Ren Leng's jade necklace and drove high into the paper necromancer's chest. One brief moment of stunned silence, the clatter of jade beads on the decking, Austin's grim smile . . .

Then a whole lotta fire.

Flaming confetti fell everywhere, ash before it touched the ground. Austin's ears rang. Everything smelled like fireworks. Austin pushed himself up from the wooden deck and blinked, vision dancing with spots. There was no sign anywhere of the Necromancer Owen Ren Leng. There never would be again.

"I'll kill you! I'll kill you if it's the last thing I do!" Victor screeched. He dragged himself kneeling from where the blast had thrown him. His hands clawed before his eyes. His right eye socket gaped empty. He pleaded, "Give it back, Austin. Give it back. You don't know . . . I'll fucking kill you!"

"You mean this?" Austin held the eye aloft. It was black as a collapsed star. Victor's head snapped toward it like a compass needle on a lodestone. "Fetch." He flung the blackened orb as far as he could, so damn far he couldn't even see the splash it made when it hit the lake.

Victor the Wizard howled and bolted after it, so mindlessly desperate that he threw himself over the deck's edge, bathrobe whipping behind him, and crashed into the water. Austin never saw him surface.

Austin ran to where JT had been thrown. He took the orc in his arms and felt for a pulse. He felt for breathing. He slapped JT's cheeks. He prayed to whatever stupid spirit ruled this place. When JT coughed, Austin went so lightheaded with relief he nearly passed out.

The Unicorn. Austin pulled the data block free from Buzz's shirt pocket (and Buzz weakly fought him, so yeah, he was all right) and held it up to the blue sky and sunlight. It rainbowed spectacularly, like it was the Hope Diamond. And as if that had been some kind of signal, the lake began to boil. Austin turned toward the sound, thinking it was Victor again, like the second ending of a bad horror sim.

It wasn't Victor. From the lake rose a giant blue bubble. It rose and kept rising until it floated in the air, a sphere of sapphire-blue water twice the size of JT's truck and emblazoned with three crossed scimitars. 3djinn had arrived, stylishly late.

CHAPTER ELEVEN

Someone was messing with JT's face. He slapped weakly in front of him and said, "Quit it," with as much threatening, slurred force as he could muster. He had a splitting headache like someone had dropped a house on him, and his eyes wouldn't focus.

Someone was saying, "Can you hear me? Hey, JT, say something."

JT's vision cleared. He was lying on a wide black leather seat that wrapped the circumference of a spherical room. The walls seemed to be made of translucent blue glass that rippled like water in a breeze. Sometimes the ripples were strong enough that a section of the walls would go clear. There wasn't a hard edge anywhere in the room. Everything was curves. There was a gap in the wall, and through it he could see the ruined face of the lodge. A ramp ran from the gap down to the deck.

"How many fingers?" Austin waved his middle finger at JT.

"Fuck you too. What happened?"

Austin held up the Blue Unicorn's data block. "I saved the day. As usual. While you sat around sleeping. As usual."

Buzz stood at a round table of black glass in the center of the room. It shimmered with aerial images and interface controls. Buzz was covered in dust and splinters and blood. He looked awful.

"Are you okay?" JT asked Buzz.

"I'm fine." Buzz came over and knelt next to JT. "You took the majority of it, I think."

"What is this place?"

"The *Marid*."

"3djinn has a magical bubble ship," Austin said.

"It's not magical."

"I don't know why they didn't just send this to San Francisco to get you."

"Maybe because it's a secret? And UFO sightings get a lot more credit these days than they used to."

JT struggled upright. He reached out to touch one of the walls. It felt like warm glass. "How does it work?"

"See, I told you he'd ask that," Austin said to Buzz. "You can't show him things like this. It gets him worked up. And then he bites."

Buzz flashed him a dirty look.

JT scanned the place closer. "I don't see any engines; how does it fly? Am I actually looking through the walls or is it a projection?"

Austin shook his head and rolled his eyes. "We probably shouldn't stick around here. Buzz, get this thing off the ground."

"No, my truck!" JT tried to stand.

Austin held him down. "JT—"

Buzz said, "Your truck is trashed, JT. Victor turned it into a pile of junk."

"I ain't leaving my truck." He pushed at Austin, but he was still a bit woozy and Austin and Buzz held him down easily.

"You can print yourself a new truck," Buzz said.

"I don't want a new truck. I want that truck."

"Hey, hey!" Austin took JT by the shoulders and turned him away from Buzz. "Hey, you know we can't stick around here long enough for you to fix it, right? We've got nothing left. We've shot our load. Wham bam, there's a good boy. And now we gotta go? Right?"

"Yeah, yeah, right." Then JT shook his head. "But maybe if I can just get it running . . . extra parts somewhere . . ." He tried once more to stand up, but Austin pushed him back down again.

"JT, your truck isn't important right now," Buzz said.

JT snarled at him, and Buzz yelped and leapt back, eyes wide.

"You're not helping!" Austin snapped at Buzz. He rubbed JT's shoulders to calm him. "I'll come back and get it for you."

"You can't even drive it."

"I'll get implants," Austin said, cheerily.

"You will not."

"I will. I'll give up magic so you can get your truck back. Fair trade, innit?"

"Shut up." Austin was just being stupid.

"Nope, it's done. No arguments. I'm getting implants." Austin sat back and looked away, feigning the end of the conversation.

JT tried to glare at Austin. He couldn't. He was filthy with zombie guts and things he didn't even want to think about. He was all battered. His drones were gone. His truck was gone. And yet, somehow, he didn't feel nearly as shitty as he should have. Austin was there beside him making stupid promises that would never come true, like old times. And JT couldn't get mad at him.

"All right. Let's go. But let's go now before I change my mind."

The Blue Unicorn's data block was heavier than it looked. A galaxy of rainbows caused by light refracting through a few million oxide monolayers danced inside it like a captured soul. JT had seen an artist who'd made window mosaics from the broken pieces of data blocks: tiny rainbows made by crystals carefully rotated and offset. It had been so beautiful, it had hurt to look at it.

It hurt to look at this block also, and JT couldn't do it anymore. He handed it to Buzz. There were no sockets on the black glass table, no data jacks, nothing. Buzz just laid the block down on it. Apparently that was enough.

"We're linked up to the 3djinn satellite. From there she can go anywhere she wants."

"3djinn has a satellite?"

Buzz shrugged. "Someone may have lost one."

Buzz wasn't an impressive-looking guy—cute, but not handsome, not striking, not scary—so it was easy to forget that he was one of the most talented hackers on the planet. Maybe he even forgot it himself. But here on this bizarre aircraft, it was hard for JT to look at Buzz and not think of all the shadows and secrets that lay behind him.

"It's starting."

JT expected to see lights or a mist or something emerge from the block and drift upward. There was nothing like that. Buzz hadn't invited JT into the *Marid*'s cyberspace to witness the transfer, so JT was as blind to what was happening as Austin. It was invisible, memory erasing itself, methodically shifting to zero-potential. To them it was just a data block on a table.

Buzz watched critically, eyes cyberspace-glazed. Austin smiled faintly, celebrating the rescue of some small part of his sister from slavery and dissection.

Austin wouldn't see this as an ending, would he? This ghost had already set a fire under him and reignited his obsession with his sister's death. People like Austin and JT never got closure. Bodies were rarely recovered when an illegal job went bad. Sometimes you didn't even know whether a person was dead or captured or just decided to say fuck it and run off. Funerals were a drink and a smoke and a toast. JT should have counted himself lucky—this was the funeral they'd never been able to give her. This wasn't a semisentient program released into the world's networks, but a soul released into whatever infinity there was.

"Goddess, I'm ready to be home," he said.

"Aaand . . . she's gone." Buzz smiled victoriously.

It was a shame that closure was just something some marketing guru had thought up to sell pop-psychology vids. It would have felt good.

Beneath them swept the Painted Desert. Mottled red and browns in the distance became sharp bands beneath them, as if they were passing over a color-coded elevation map and not real geography. The walls of the *Marid* never remained transparent for long; ripples of black and blue passed over the view.

Buzz and JT sat together and watched everything roll past. JT said, "You aren't going to stay with me, are you? You'd be safe there."

"Seeing you and Austin talking again, I thought that meant you were putting together a new team and maybe you wanted me along, you know, like you needed Roan, someone net-side doing that part of the job. And in my head I was thinking all this was like an interview or a test run or something. And you and I, we could kind of be like how you and—" He broke off talking with a nervous glance at Austin because Austin was right there. But Austin pretended he hadn't heard any of it, so Buzz went on, "But you ain't putting together a team are you?"

"No. I'm going home. And Austin's going back to wherever Austin goes."

"Those years Roan and I roomed together, I knew what she did when she ran with you guys and you all left on your jobs and I stayed home by myself and did my thing. I was an accountant. I moved numbers from one column to another until they told the story I wanted them to tell. I was good at it. But nobody knew who I was. And, meanwhile, you all were fucking superheroes. I know I'd be safe with you." He looked away from JT, through the rippling walls to the world outside. "I don't want to be safe."

And JT understood. Of course he understood. If someone had asked him to quit while he'd been on that high after that first job they'd all done together six years ago, JT would have said the same thing. And though he didn't feel it now, he remembered that high, and he remembered he and Austin had gotten drunk and stoned and had fucked like animals all night. There wasn't going to be any fucking this time, was there?

JT said, "With everything that's happened, I never got to say thank you."

"For what?"

"For Jason Taylor. For giving me the chance to be someone else."

Buzz leaned in and gave him a soft bittersweet kiss good-bye. "Same."

Austin watched JT watch the strange blue globe fly off north. JT looked melancholy, but then, JT always looked melancholy.

"Were you actually in love with him?"

"No. But I wanted to be."

The globe didn't seem to move, not like a plane. It only shrank until it was gone.

"It doesn't matter," JT said. "It's hardly my first rodeo gone bad."

"Maybe it will be the last."

"Yeah, sure."

Austin slung his bags over his shoulder, and the two of them crossed the lot of JT's compound toward the house.

Dante burst out of the garage where she lived. She pointed at the sky and shouted and danced around like she was on fire. "What the fuck was that? Did you just come out of that? What was that? Was that aliens? I knew there was aliens, man! I knew it! Did you go to Mars? You went to fucking Mars, didn't you? Or Europa or Io or some fucking place. Can I tell anyone? Is this like some secret that if I tell anyone they'll wipe my memory or something? I won't tell a soul, man, not a fucking soul, I swear. Except Duke, what do I tell Duke? Because he's been wanting to know where the hell you been, and I told him I don't know. Fucking don't get wi-fi on Mars, do ya? Fuckin' right ya don't. Holy fuck, what was that? I want to go to Mars!"

"Hi, Dante," JT said.

"We didn't go to Mars," Austin said.

Dante went from pointing upward to pointing at Austin like she hadn't even noticed Austin was there until he'd spoken. "What's . . ." Dante stopped herself and finished her accusation with a pained look that evidently Austin wasn't meant to understand.

Austin understood just fine. Adoptive father and daughter were reuniting, and no place for Austin. "I'll be inside." He adjusted his bags and glared at Dante. As he brushed past the young orc, he snapped his arm like he was going to throw a punch.

Dante jumped back. "You see that!"

"He's just messing with you. Don't worry. He's leaving."

Austin kept walking. "Yeah," he muttered to himself, "Don't worry. I'm leaving."

Suddenly he couldn't get out of there fast enough.

So why didn't he leave, then? Just to draw out the pain, he supposed.

Austin showered, repacked his things, and still JT hadn't come in from talking with Dante, so he unpacked again and ran laundry. He poked around the house.

Living room, dining room, and kitchen all one big room. The front of the house was photosensitive glass, curtainless and tinted amber by the afternoon sun. There was nothing in the house that said that once upon a time JT had been one of the most notorious data thieves in Pacifica. Nothing that hinted at Austin or Grayson or Roan or Bell Anderson. Nothing that said anything about JT except that he was a technophile with a taste for minimalist decor and exposed concrete.

Austin sat on the couch and drifted off into a sleeping trance. Nebraska came and nudged at him, but then went away.

Movement stirred him awake. JT had gone into the john and left the door open a crack, a bachelor's habit. Austin heard the thunder of JT pissing. It gave Austin that vague butterfly feeling and stirred up an ache thinking of the dick that could make a stream that loud. Then he heard the hiss of the shower, and all Austin had to do was move two meters and he could have watched JT strip down through the crack in the door. He didn't.

He went to the fridge and rooted for food. Either Dante had eaten everything since they'd been gone, or there'd been nothing but condiments there in the first place. Probably everything would have had meat in it anyway. He threw his clothes in the dryer.

An hour later, JT came out of the bathroom wearing a clean pair of jeans and pulling down a steam-dampened T-shirt that clung to him like paint. He wasn't wearing underwear. Though his jeans weren't tight, Austin knew what to look for: that thick fold of denim there along his thigh was the curve of his cock; that faint shadow was the ridge of its head. God, Austin needed to be out of here.

JT sniffed himself. "Nearly boiled my skin off and I still smell like zombie."

"It's in your head. You smell like Lave-Love Springtime scent. There are other soaps, you know. Some of them actually smell like springtime."

JT shook his head. "I smell zombie." He went back into the bathroom, used a towel to pick up his fouled clothes, and dropped the whole mess into the kitchen incinerator. He opened the refrigerator, grunted, then squirted mustard on a heel of bread. He ate it at the front window.

Anyone else would have thought he was watching the sun set. Austin knew JT was watching the change in light over the Corvette.

Austin leaned against the dryer. It hummed against the small of his back. "The kid knows who I am, doesn't she? She knows who you are. She know everything?"

"Yeah. Not every last detail. Enough. She knows what we've done."

And JT didn't say sex or thieving or killing, so Austin assumed he meant all of the above. "You trust her that much?"

"Yeah. I do. But it wasn't like that. It wasn't like I said, 'Sit down, I got something to tell ya.' We were drunk one night and talking and elves came up and so we started talking about elves 'cause she'd never met one growing up in Greentown, just seen them a couple of times, and I told her about you and how . . .'"

And that was more than just a trailing off. That was JT deciding he didn't want to finish that thought.

Austin was about to press him: *How what, JT?* but JT said, "And I told her about you and then everything else."

"You talked about elves, and then you talked about me because you don't know any other elves, and then 'everything else'? And that's why you blew your cover to a seventeen-year-old car thief?"

"Yeah."

You're the worst fucking liar in the world. Austin didn't know which words were the lie exactly, or maybe they were all lies, or maybe half-truths or whatever, but there was lying in there somewhere. And maybe it was a bit hypocritical, because Austin knew he wasn't always so truthful either, but it stung that JT would lie to him. "She's that special?"

"This whole life is special."

JT didn't look at him when he said that, and that's how Austin knew it was true, and how Austin knew that he really had to go.

JT took a tiny bite from his sad little sandwich and stared out at the blacker-than-black car. He changed the subject. Or maybe in his head it wasn't a subject change at all. "Dante says everything's ready for the big meeting tomorrow. This is it, ya know, our first big break. I mean, we haven't done bad so far, but it's all been small orders except for the rigs we've put together for Duke and his mercs, but he's an investor, so that doesn't count. But Suborbital . . . Our first big break."

Austin didn't say anything. What could he say? He hoped the meeting would fail.

JT took another bite of his sandwich, grimaced at it, and tossed what was left on the dining table.

Austin knew JT wouldn't fail. JT was a genius. JT and Dante would do their song and dance in front of the Suborbital execs, and they'd win themselves a contract worth hundreds of millions and that would be that.

JT chose a plastic mesh ball cap from a rack of them and went outside. Austin watched JT walk to the car. JT opened the door with his mind and climbed into the driver's seat. Austin thought that JT would take the car for one last drive, but he didn't. He just sat there.

The timer on the clothes dryer buzzed.

Austin went outside to tell JT good-bye.

"Thinking?" The driver's-side window was down. JT was sitting inside, eyes closed, looking like he was meditating.

"No. Just enjoying the breeze."

"From inside the car?"

"I am the car."

A long streamlined curve ran from front fender to rear. Austin brushed his fingers along the stretch of it beneath the window. The special paint of the car absorbed radiation, so the car was still warm from the daytime sun even though the air had started to cool. "You can feel that?"

JT didn't open his eyes or turn to look. He nodded. "The ridge under the window."

"What's it feel like?" It was a question he always asked about the way JT experienced the world. Machine sensoria was something that many took for granted, but was something Austin would never know. JT always answered unhelpfully, *It feels like feeling.* Except this time he said, "It feels nice."

Austin swiped a hand lightly over the car top. "Does it all feel the same?"

"No."

So Austin walked around the car, running his hand along the curves and angles and lines of the fender, the bumper, the spoiler. He kept going, and at the front of the car, he traced the chrome of the headlights with his thumb and rattled his fingers across the grille. Through the windshield's tinting, he could make out the dark outline of JT's jaw and the ball cap he was never without, and he could see the faint red glow of arousal in JT's eyes. It didn't all feel the same, did it? Some of it felt much, much better.

Front and center of the car's hood gleamed the Corvette emblem in chrome, red, and black: crossed racing flags stylized into a V. Austin knelt before it, eyes locked on the burning eyes inside. If this didn't work, he would look like a complete fool. Well, some things were worth the risk, weren't they?

Austin ran his tongue slowly along one edge of the emblem. Chrome and lacquer tasted like nothing at all. He ran his tongue along the opposite edge.

He glanced up. JT's head was thrown back against the headrest. His eyes were closed, lips parted in a small O. Austin smiled. Sometimes it paid to look foolish.

Austin made love to the emblem with his tongue. It was the most ridiculous thing he had ever done. He wouldn't have done it if he hadn't known that JT didn't find it ridiculous at all.

Austin swept his tongue over the flags. He dabbed at them and traced around them. He stroked one side with his fingertips while he licked the other. He did whatever came to mind, having no idea what worked and what didn't, all of it feeling equally silly. And what did it feel like to JT? A blowjob? A rimjob? To a guy with a car fetish, maybe it felt like something incomparable.

"Austin?" JT growled softly. "Austin, come here."

Austin ignored him. It was always best to ignore JT. The orc never really knew what he wanted until Austin showed him.

Enjoying the breeze, JT had said. The emblem was wet from Austin's spit. He blew it dry. He licked and he blew.

"Austin!"

Austin went around to the driver's side. He was going to say something smart-ass, but JT reached out the window and caught his belt and pulled him hard and tight against the car door with a thump. He held Austin there with one hand and undid Austin's belt and khakis with the other. A thrill shot through Austin. A thrill even better than seeing Nebraska pluck that eye out of Victor's head. This was what Austin had been missing the last two years. This was what he wanted.

JT's warm, soft mouth sucked him in. JT's tongue stroked him and swirled. Austin knew the satisfaction of feeling a cock swell slowly in your mouth, and he wanted JT to feel that too. So he fought the shiver that ran through him and the blood that coursed down. He tried to slow his heart rate and his breath. He wanted everything slow.

But he'd wanted this for too long, not just from the moment he'd driven into the compound and seen JT in his grease-covered overalls, but long before that. Forever before that. And Austin, who could run barefoot over a forest floor covered in knives of ice and ignore the pain, couldn't ignore what JT was doing. He was rock-hard in moments.

JT's arm snaked around Austin's waist and held him fast. Austin couldn't move if he wanted to. He stretched his arms forward over the roof of the car and laid his cheek against the smooth warm plastic.

It felt dirty and exciting, getting sucked off out in the open like this. Like he was one of the prostitutes down at Volunteer Park giving his dick to some john who didn't want to leave his car. He glanced over to the big garage, half expecting Dante to be standing there watching. Dante wasn't. Lights flickered inside through windows and doors open to the night.

JT covered Austin's nuts with warmth, then cooled them with a hiss of breath, the same as Austin had done to the crossed-flags emblem. Yeah, that had worked just as he'd thought. The warmth of the car, the cool breeze on the back of his neck, the rocklike heat of JT's arm around him, the soft tongue prodding Austin's balls, tugging, sucking, fangs and tusks catching and nipping, the contrast of all these sensations—warm and cool, soft and firm, dull and sharp—made Austin shiver. He whispered JT's name as heat slowly blossomed through him: JT. JT.

JT took him in again, and Austin felt the soft head of his cock press against the softness at the back of JT's mouth and then slide on down, JT's throat snug around him and so warm. All of him was in JT now.

JT fucked his own throat with Austin's cock, insistent, needing, as rough on himself as he was on Austin, like what he really wanted was to shove all of Austin inside him and eat him alive, cock and balls first.

Like a dying star, the bloom of heat that wracked Austin hit critical mass. Austin Shea, greatest fuck on the western seaboard, wasn't going to last even ten minutes with JT sucking him. It would have been shameful if it hadn't been mind-erasing first. The bloom trembled. Austin tried to push away from the car. He wanted to watch. JT's arm held him like a steel band. Austin fought him and JT let go, growling, unhappy.

Austin came, one arm on the edge of the roof keeping his head from smacking down. His body contracted tight, contracted, and contracted like a black hole forming inside him. "JT," Austin said as his spunk splashed on JT's forehead and nose and cheek and the rack of it all drove through him. "JT."

A long time later he looked down. JT was resting his chin on his arm on the window's edge, smiling faintly, all tusks and spunk, looking happier than Austin had seen him since forever.

Austin swiped a finger through his seed as it started to slide into JT's narrow trail of a beard. JT opened his mouth, and Austin let him suck his finger clean. JT's tongue on Austin's finger felt every bit as good as JT's tongue on Austin's cock. He pulled his finger out. *Pop.*

"More," JT said. So Austin kept feeding him.

"More."

"Ain't no more."

"So make more." JT gave him a pissed-off look, like that should have been obvious.

Austin ran his hand along his cock. JT's eyes opened to slits, red as laser light, hungry, and watched Austin jack himself. People always thought an elf's cock should be pretty, elegant somehow. Austin's wasn't. It was like the root of some old tree, ridged and gnarled and wrapped in veins. It was a great cock for sucking. Hell, it was a great cock for anything. He made sure JT got a good view of it as he stroked. And the look on JT's face got hungrier and hungrier.

JT glanced up at him. "You brought protection?"

"Protection from what?" Austin smiled coyly. His hand made slick noises as he smeared JT's spit over his cock.

"I want you to fuck me."

"Yeah?"

"Yeah."

"We don't need protection."

"Yes, we do." Wetness crackled as Austin stroked.

"Glove compartment."

JT popped the dash and drew out a pair of oversized tungsten handcuffs. They couldn't be bothered to make clothes or cars sized for orcs. But they sure could make handcuffs. "Good. Now get in the car."

CHAPTER TWELVE

Austin looked inside the car. JT barely fit in the driver's seat as it was. Sex in that car wouldn't be hot; it would be cramped and someone would get an elbow in the eye. "Get out."

JT glowered at him.

"Come on."

The door swept up, and JT climbed out. He winced and tried to adjust himself, but there was no adjusting something like that. Austin was surprised that JT hadn't already split the seams of his jeans apart. "Don't bother," Austin said as JT struggled to get everything unpinched. "Just strip."

JT plucked at the hem of his shirt, hesitant. Austin didn't know whether he was being coy or bashful.

"I said strip."

JT slowly peeled the tight shirt up over his head.

Too much pizza and beer and not enough action had put a few pounds on JT. The four-pack abs he'd had two years ago had lost all their definition, and JT was obviously embarrassed. JT had always been so damn touchy about his body, as if most people wouldn't kill for a body like that, green or not. Austin could never say anything, not one compliment, not even that he liked the extra weight.

And he did like it. He liked it a lot. And he liked the trail of black hair down the stomach. And he liked JT's absurdly broad chest, a little less ripped now than it had been, but still fanned with black hair. And he liked his tiny nipples, hard and black as obsidian. And the branching thick veins on JT's shoulders and biceps, knotting on down to his oversized hands, Austin liked all that too. And he liked watching the cloth of the T-shirt stretch over all that muscle as if it would tear.

Finally the T-shirt was off and fell to the pavement hopelessly stretched out of shape by the body it had hugged.

"Jeans," Austin prompted.

JT worked his jeans off his hips and slid them down. He pushed the thick rod of his cock down with them. When it finally snapped free, it bobbed heavily. JT let the jeans fall and stepped out of them. And there he was, buck naked, and all for Austin.

Green skin, tusks, and glowing eyes aside, no one would ever mistake JT for a human or elf. His shoulders were half again as broad as Austin's, his arms twice as thick, but his waist just as narrow. His arms were too long, his legs were too short, his hands and feet were too big. And his cock and balls were just as out of proportion as the rest of him.

"Turn around." So JT did.

Christ, would you look at that beautiful ass? Yeah, JT had put on some weight. Perfect weight. Exactly the weight he had needed to fill out. There was an ass ready for marking.

JT blushed and looked over his shoulder at Austin. "Your turn to strip. My turn to stare."

He turned back and watched Austin strip. Where JT looked, Austin felt it like a touch.

People had ideas about how an elf should look: narrow-built, long slender muscles, eternally boyish if not just plain feminine, a teenager never quite coming into manhood, Donatello's *David* instead of Michelangelo's. Every striation of muscle showed on Austin's body. Every major vein roped thick over him, not just his hands and his forearms, but twisting over his biceps, where shoulders met chest, and down his abdomen like ivy over a tree. Austin's skin seemed so thin and tight it could tear. And everywhere glossy purple and white scars crisscrossed him.

JT ran a thumb along one of Austin's newer scars. "You hurt yourself more."

Austin shivered and goose bumps rose beneath the touch. "To be fair, I wasn't trying to get hurt."

JT traced another. Two years since JT had seen Austin naked, and JT knew which of the scores of marks on Austin's body were new and which ones were not. One after another, he touched the new ones. "When are you going to stop?"

Replies logjammed in Austin's head. *Never, it's what I was made for. Never, until I learn the truth. Never, if it means you'll keep touching me like you're doing now. Never.*

JT traced a black-nailed finger down Austin, through the thin dusting of fine glossy pubic hair, soft and light brown, and he wrapped his oversized hand around Austin's hard cock covering all but a few centimeters. JT's fingers were rough from work, like fine sandpaper. He pulled his hand gently down the length of Austin and ran his thumb over the reddened head.

Austin brushed JT's hand with his own. They never held hands. It seemed like there had been a time they used to kiss, but they didn't anymore. And, just now, looking into JT's eyes and seeing the dark-red burn there and needing him more than he ever had, Austin couldn't remember why the two of them never did those things. He tried to entwine his fingers through JT's, but JT jerked his hand away. "How do you want me?" JT said.

"Bent over the hood."

JT glanced over his shoulder at Dante's garage. Lights flickered inside. Where they stood now, the car blocked the view. On the hood, there'd be nothing keeping Dante from catching an eyeful.

Austin said, "Your kid's busy building herself a man or a spaceship or whatever she's building in there. Besides, don't tell me she's never caught you fucking before."

JT spread his legs and leaned over the front of the car, catching himself with his hands on the hood. His cock and balls swung. He lowered himself until his face rested against the black molded plastic. He put his hands behind his back so all his weight was on his neck. It couldn't have been comfortable, but that was okay. Austin didn't want him comfortable.

Austin moved behind him and right here, right now, was almost the vision Austin had teased himself with two days ago: balls and cock hanging heavy and low so Austin could get to them if he wanted, and that beautiful green ass parted just enough to show JT's tight hole ringed in black hair.

Austin cuffed him. The ratchet sound brought a fantasy of them playing cops and robbers. But Austin as the cop was just too silly, and there was no need for fantasies anymore. JT was right here.

He crouched between JT's legs. He bit the tender inside of JT's thigh, and JT jumped. He bit the other thigh. He licked upward, cheek brushing against shaved nuts, and sucked hard at JT's taint. He slapped JT on his ass, one cheek, then the other, as he sucked and licked the space between asshole and ball sack. The slaps drew pink up into the green. They turned his ass that blended autumn color Austin liked so much. Austin's other hand slid around JT's massive nuts. He twisted and pulled. JT growled and bucked his hips back, everything available and ready, and Austin buried his face deep.

His tongue lapped at JT's hole. It clenched tight, then loosened, then clenched again. And there was nothing that smelled like JT. All orcs had a strong smell to them, yeah, but JT smelled like springtime soap and clean sweat and a loamy musk so strong it made Austin dizzy. It made him feel like he was buried alive in warm earth rich with magic.

He slid his tongue into JT's hole and pried him open. He flicked at it, sucked at the edges of it, and all the while he kneaded that fine ass with one hand and roughed up JT's balls with the other. Used to be he could get JT close just from tugging and squeezing his balls, the harder the better. And from the sounds JT was making and his pre-come already beading from loose foreskin, that hadn't changed. JT writhed under him. Tungsten links clicked together. Austin fucked him with his tongue and sucked and bit at his ass and squeezed and pulled harder on those nuts until the skin of his sack stretched thin and shiny.

He slicked up a finger with spit and slid it into JT's ass, hot and so goddamn tight Austin would never get his cock in there. He twisted the finger, and then drove two fingers in. JT's whole body shook. JT whined and growled and adjusted his stance and forced his ass up high, squirming to get Austin deeper. Austin finger-fucked him, twisting and pulling at the tight ring of his hole, trying to loosen it up.

He stuffed one of JT's nuts into his mouth and pulled until it popped free.

"Austin, please . . ." he heard JT whisper between harsh breaths.

"Please what?" Austin drove his fingers deeper.

"Fuck me."

"You're still too tight."

"Then hurt me."

Austin sat back on his heels and admired the blush of pink he'd brought to JT's ass and the bruising he'd brought to his nuts. He took JT's massive cock and milked it and got himself a handful of slickness. He lubed up his dick and ran another swipe of it at JT's tight hole. He stood and pressed the head of his cock against it.

"Say that again."

"Hurt me," JT whispered.

And it was so damn tempting to do just that, shove it on in hard and fast and let JT howl and curse him. It would serve JT right for being an asshole two nights ago. It would serve JT right for being an asshole for two years. A good grudge fuck would do Austin good. A good grudge fuck would make it easier to leave when it was all over with.

So of course he didn't do that. He pushed in nice and firm and stroked JT's sides and back to calm him.

JT clenched up anyway. Every muscle locked rigid. His ass pinched tight.

"Fuck, JT, give it up," Austin hissed at him. And he wondered how long it had been since JT had let a guy do this to him. He'd assumed JT had a parade of men waiting for him. Maybe he'd assumed wrong.

JT relaxed one hitched breath at a time, and Austin sank in slowly. He liked watching himself sink in, forcing that beautiful puckered green ass open, stretching it wide to swallow him up one knot and vein at a time. JT's breath came in a shallow, jerking whine. It sounded like pain. It looked like pain the way his shoulders and arms tensed and released, but he pushed his ass back onto Austin. Pain or not, JT wanted it. So Austin kept on, and that tight ring of muscle slid down, around, and over him. The heat of JT's insides engulfed him. Heat better than heaven. And then JT was snug around the base of Austin's cock and Austin was deep as he could go.

He kept pushing. He forced JT down against the car hood until JT had to give up on standing. JT crashed down on the hood with a thump as his feet came up.

Austin lay across JT's impossibly broad back and stayed buried in him. JT rose and fell beneath Austin, all ragged breathing. His cuffed hands squirmed between their bodies. The metal cuffs bit into Austin's stomach.

Austin licked along JT's ears. "Look at me, JT. Let me see your eyes." JT turned his head and opened his eyes, sleepily, drunkenly, tripping high on Austin's glamour. They were flecked with orange, and the flecks dimmed and brightened and swam slowly in the glittering black. Austin ground his hips side to side against JT. JT's eyes narrowed and the flecks swam like bonfire sparks reflected in dark water. JT was ready.

Austin fucked him good and slow, a little bit in, a little bit out. Heaven: that tight ring sliding over his cock, up and down, tightening, loosening; the soft heat past that. JT's chest rumbled under Austin, the purring sound JT made and didn't even know he made it, like JT was a finely tuned, old-time car. Austin liked that idea: finally, a car Austin could drive better than anyone. Right here: first gear. He liked first gear. He could do this all night if he wanted. He could pop a couple of times, good slow pops.

Not tonight. If Austin had to leave, if this was the last time, then Austin wanted to see JT lose control. When Austin drove off into the sunset, JT needed to know what he was losing.

Sweat sucked between his chest and JT's back as Austin lifted himself, arms straight. He fucked a bit deeper, a bit harder, and now each drive home made JT grunt, broke his purr up. JT's hands clenched and released just like his ass did around Austin's cock. Austin shifted and planted both hands on the small of JT's back and fucked with his hips. Yeah, that was a good angle there. Feel that ass slip around him, giving over to Austin. *Yeah, you missed this, JT. You missed this.*

JT growled Austin's name, and that was his cue to lean into it, harder. *Put your back into it, Austin.* Skin slapping, now. Breaking a sweat.

"Austin, let me go." Third gear, now. Harder. Ball-slapping. Make him feel it, every goddamn centimeter of it. "Austin, you fucker, let me go. Austin, it's my turn. Austin, let me go, you fuck." JT jerked at the handcuffs. The muscles of his arms bunched and his back went rigid with the strain of trying to break free. JT growled a string of half-finished thoughts: "Austin, stop. Goddess. Austin, let me go. You can't make me . . . come . . . going to fuck you . . . bloody . . . Austin . . . make you . . . oh goddess . . . oh fuck . . . Austin . . . stop . . . you can't . . . fuck me!"

Austin pulled out, all the way out. And the desert night air was so cool on his cock, cool as winter outside of JT. "That what you want?"

And JT looked over his shoulder and roared at him, mindless, fangs flashing, eyes dripping fire.

"That's what I thought." And Austin slammed back inside him, bone-jarring hard. JT bucked and kicked and fought against the handcuffs as if he wanted Austin to stop, as if he'd kill Austin if he ever broke free, but Austin knew better.

What visions did he see lost so deep in Austin's glamour? Did he even know it was Austin inside him, fucking him apart? Or had JT become nothing but orc lust and hunger and violence?

Austin fought him. He drove harder, deep as he could, breathing harsh, sweating heavy. His cock felt electric, his balls felt heavy, filled with warm lead, and the warmth spreading. He leaned into JT, one hand on JT's shoulder blade, the other on the back of his neck, shoving him down against the car with his whole body on each fuck, forcing a JT-shaped dent into the plastic.

The wildfire in his cock and balls built and spread, and it wasn't just the sensations of fucking, not just his cock deep in JT's ass, or JT's thick musk and sweat, or skin like satin and muscles like steel under Austin's hands. It was the rush of power he felt with JT crazed under him. Like riding a wild animal. Like regaining control over a spun-out car. JT beneath Austin, bucking and roaring: it had been Austin who had driven him to that and Austin who'd tamed him. And that made Austin feel like a fucking god.

JT gave in. Just like that, he stopped fighting. He collapsed beneath Austin, howling softly and pitifully like he was dying. He whispered, "Austin, Austin, Austin, Austin, please."

That was too much, and the leaden fire broke white and erasing, and Austin burst inside JT and filled him. Gasping, sweat pouring from him, heart hammering, he kept fucking, cock slipping through the thick cream he pumped into JT, shoving it deeper, pulling it out in a slick white mess, pumping out more. He kept fucking until he stopped shaking and could breathe again and see again.

He wasn't finished. There'd be time to catch his breath later.

Austin pulled JT down to the front of the car and rolled him onto his back. JT's cuffed hands were beneath his ass, raising it to just the right height. Austin held JT's legs in the air by the ankles and slid back into him. He shoved the pain of hypersensitivity aside like he would a knife wound. And he started all over again, JT's turn this time.

He watched JT as he fucked. He watched JT's nuts—one to each side of his thick cock—bob with each thrust. He watched the pre-come drizzle from JT's thick foreskin, the head of his cock still hidden inside. His eyes tracked the sweat beading on JT's forehead and trickling into his matted black hair as his head rolled left and right. He watched JT's eyes flicker with need, glowing phosphorescent orange. And Austin kept fucking, wet and noisy.

Broad chest all banded muscle, olive green, malachite green, agate and jade, dusted with short black hair. Narrow abdomen, no ripples anymore, trail of hair, slick and glittering with sweat and JT's own juice. Austin could smell the rank, wet leaf, loam-scent of JT growing stronger. Austin fucked faster, sensitivity past, ready again.

He leaned down over his orc. Sweat dripped from his nose onto JT's throat and ran down one side of JT's neck over veins and rigid tendons. *His* orc. JT *was* Austin's orc. JT had always been Austin's orc from day one, and one of these days JT would admit it. "Come for me, JT. Show me what you can do." And he ground his hips hard into JT and felt himself swell larger, ready to blow for the second time.

Austin leaned back, wanting to watch as JT's body locked, arched and rigid. His arms strained against the handcuffs, biceps twice the size of softballs, veins bulging. His head smacked into the car's hood, and he roared, tusks and fangs and teeth all showing. His cock swelled longer and thicker, finally enough for all that foreskin to slip, and there was his pinkish-green head, and it busted everywhere. Thick white fountained, and spray splattered past JT's head and ran down the windshield. It fell into sweat-matted hair and streaked his face and kept on coming, more and more of it. JT's jaws clacked shut, lips peeled back from fangs and teeth, unable to scream anymore, unable to breathe or do anything but come.

And his ass went tight as a vise around Austin, so tight that when Austin came, it hurt to push all that load through his clamped-down cock. *Tell me you're not mine,* Austin thought through his own pulsing haze. *Tell me anyone else can do to you what I just did. Tell me you don't need me. Tell me you haven't missed me and don't want me back, and I'll tell you you're a fucking liar.*

Their chests heaved. Austin pulled out of JT slowly, pulling a trickle of come with him and then a splash when his head popped free. It ran and pooled along the edges of the crossed-flags emblem. JT, eyes closed, groaned and frowned like a sleeping cat who didn't like to be messed with. Austin smirked, satisfied with the glorious mess he'd made: the big green man was exhausted and soaked in sweat and practically drowned in his own cooling come. The hood ran with sweat and all else. It was dented, and there were deep scratches where the handcuffs and JT's tusks had scored through the enamel. Austin wondered if JT had been linked to the car through all that. Had it hurt, or had it been some kind of ecstasy Austin couldn't imagine?

Austin's eyes slid to his clothes lying scattered on the concrete and his cocky smile faded. It was over now, wasn't it? He picked up his clothes and walked back to the house, leaving JT dazed on the hood of the car. Had he really thought one more fuck was going to change things between them? In the history of everything, when had that ever worked?

Austin folded clothes warm from the dryer and stuffed them into his gym bag. Why had he brought so many goddamn shirts?

"Where are you going?" JT said sleepily from the door.

"San Francisco."

"Now?"

"Yes."

Austin folded a shirt into thirds and then rolled it. JT hadn't said anything or moved, so Austin turned to look at him. JT was still naked. He was still damp with come. His hands were still cuffed behind his back.

"Oh shit. Sorry." He went over to JT and tapped the code on the cuffs. JT's wrists were abraded all to hell. Austin tossed the cuffs on the table next to the barely eaten mustard sandwich and returned to his folding.

JT went to his bedroom. He stopped at the door and said, "You should stay."

"I really think I shouldn't."

"You can leave in the morning."

Austin stopped folding, a flash of anger. *And how will that make anything better?* he wanted to say.

"Sleep with me. In my bed. With me." And he disappeared into his room.

Austin's heart raced. He glanced down at his hands. The shirt he'd been folding was wrung into a twist. He tried to tell himself all the reasons why he shouldn't do this, but though the reasons were there, the words for them never came. He dropped the hopelessly wrinkled shirt into the laundry basket and went to the door of JT's bedroom.

JT had an iron-framed bed. Thrown over it were woolen blankets dyed in Southwest First People's patterns: turquoise blue and carnelian red. JT was sprawled naked on top of them, malachite green.

Austin took the last few steps to the bed and sat on the edge. JT pulled him down. His arms folded around him and engulfed him. He spooned around the back of him, cold, sticky come and sweat pressed between them. His tusks scraped at the back of Austin's neck and caught in his hair.

When they'd gone into hiding after escaping the wizards' laboratory, they'd lain together like this. In a dark basement of an abandoned building, on an old, bare mattress thrown on the floor in the corner, they'd huddled together and watched the door of the damp, moldy room, knowing that at any moment the wizards would appear there and take them again. And JT, who could smell fear, had said, "You're not afraid. It makes me think we have a chance."

Austin lay there with JT's massive arms around him, arms that could break him but would never do that. It had been Austin who'd come up with the handcuffs, but they'd always been for show. They'd been to make JT feel safe, not Austin. These arms would never hurt him. One slid down to his waist. JT's hand wrapped around Austin's balls snug and warm.

And Austin hadn't been afraid in that basement. He'd been on edge and nervous, but not afraid. Because JT had been holding him exactly the way he was holding Austin now, and nothing could hurt him while JT held him that way. Nothing could hurt either of them so long as they held each other.

This had been a terrible mistake. Austin should go.

Men never stayed. So JT wasn't used to a man in his bed, let alone holding one so tightly against him. He couldn't sleep this way. He made a virtual round of his home checking doors and windows. He stretched his senses beyond the house and into the grounds. Turret cameras showed dark desert. He cycled through infrared and ultraviolet and saw only a fox.

There was nothing to do but be with Austin, though he didn't know how. He couldn't sleep this way, but he wouldn't let go, either. He drifted in and out of sleep, the reality of Austin's perfect body against him mixing with strange dreams, leftover glamour visions of smoking battlefields smelling like hot road, and JT comfortably dying, speared through by an incomparable elf.

JT's ass was sore. His hole burned a little, tingled a little. It felt stretched out and tight as a rubber band all at once. It would feel like that for a day. His cock was tucked along the crack of Austin's ass, harder than ever, but right now JT didn't want any more than this here. Maybe in the morning he'd take Austin the way Austin had taken him.

Maybe that's what was making Austin nervous. JT could smell the anxiety on him.

And Austin also smelled like sex: like gym sweat, and the clean soapy smell of all their mingled come. JT licked the back of Austin's neck. He tasted the salt there and got himself high off the faint scent in his hair: battlefield smoke, hot road, glamour.

It had taken a week for JT to fall in love with Austin way back when. Another week to realize that Austin didn't love him back. That for Austin, the sex had just been sex. And then a year for JT to convince himself he had only thought he was in love. It had just been the glamour. Austin's glamour was a beautiful, strange, and frightening lie constantly whispering into JT's ear.

Like just now: it was so easy to imagine the two of them like this always. Too easy. He should tell Austin to go. He would tell him. In just a few minutes. He could stand to listen to the lie just a few minutes more.

Neither of them moved. Austin didn't go. JT slept and held and listened.

EPILOGUE

Dante's ex was Mathew Carter. He'd been nothing but trouble, goading her on, promising her sex and drugs and love if Dante would only do everything he asked. *"Just a little more money, baby, and that's the last time you gotta steal for me."* Every week he'd said that. Every week she'd believed him.

So, okay, she couldn't blame everything on him. There'd been the drugs, and she'd have jacked those cars with or without him, but he hadn't helped none either. And it wasn't until Jason Taylor (the infamous JT) had knocked some sense into her head—literally knocked some sense into her head—and shown her what Mathew was doing, that Dante had had the strength to leave him and the drugs and move on. It was JT who'd showed her that, so Dante owed JT her life. It was simple as that.

And, yeah, so it was naïve to look up to JT the way she did. JT wasn't no fucking saint, after all. Dante knew that. Dante knew JT was a thief and a killer. She knew all the rest. And Dante knew it was ninety percent jealousy she was feeling just now. JT was going to start spending all his time with that elf and less time with her until JT forgot all about Dante Riggs. She'd seen it before, dozens of times. Her mother had gone chasing off after whatever boyfriend had been the flavor of the week and forgot all about Dante every time. She knew how it was.

And so it hurt—goddamn, it hurt—to watch JT fall into that fucking elf's trap. Because Mathew and that elf, they were the same kind of people: users and liars. JT couldn't see it because JT was too close (Or maybe it was because of elf magic just like JT told her.

Hadn't JT been the one to warn her?), but Dante could see it. Dante saw it all perfectly clear.

And she felt a little guilty for watching them fuck, but, Christ, they'd been doing it right there in the lot, so how could she not fucking see? They might as well have put up a goddamn sign.

Well, it was a sign, wasn't it? That had been JT's way of calling for help, Dante was sure. Dante could save him. She just had to think of a way to get that elf gone for good.

Dante spun on a wheeled office chair in the printer control booth and brainstormed. The 210-centimeter monitors all held a rotating view of the vehicle she'd been designing—her journeyman's project. The main holo projector on the floor threw up a blue 3-D life-sized projection of it. It still had a long way to go; she had a lot left to learn. Dante hadn't so much as glanced at it in over an hour. She spun the chair and thought.

The door of her holographic vehicle swung open and out stepped a woman.

Dante nearly shit herself. It wasn't supposed to do that. It wasn't animated at all. She jumped up so fast that the chair shot out behind her. This was some prank of JT's. But JT would never have messed with her project. Not ever. And she could feel the woman's presence blossom into the compound's cyberspace, and she could feel the woman's melancholy tug at her heart.

The woman said, "Help me, Dante Riggs. You're my only hope."

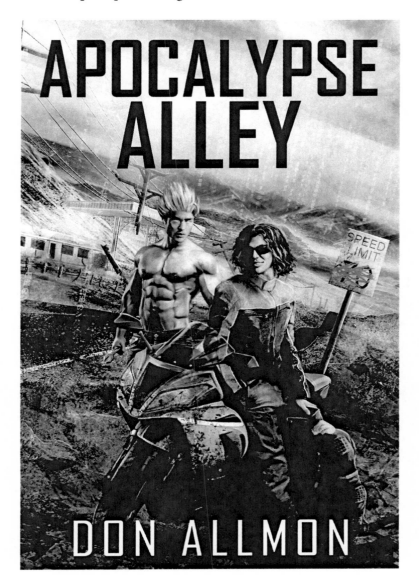

APOCALYPSE ALLEY

DON ALLMON

Dear Reader,

Thank you for reading Don Allmon's *The Glamour Thieves*!

We know your time is precious and you have many, many entertainment options, so it means a lot that you've chosen to spend your time reading. We really hope you enjoyed it.

We'd be honored if you'd consider posting a review—good or bad—on sites like **Amazon, Barnes & Noble, Kobo, Goodreads, Twitter, Facebook, Tumblr,** and your blog or website. We'd also be honored if you told your friends and family about this book. Word of mouth is a book's lifeblood!

For more information on upcoming releases, author interviews, blog tours, contests, giveaways, and more, please sign up for our weekly, spam-free newsletter and visit us around the web:

Newsletter: tinyurl.com/RiptideSignup
Twitter: twitter.com/RiptideBooks
Facebook: facebook.com/RiptidePublishing
Goodreads: tinyurl.com/RiptideOnGoodreads
Tumblr: riptidepublishing.tumblr.com

Thank you so much for Reading the Rainbow!

RiptidePublishing.com

ACKNOWLEDGMENTS

I'd like to thank Barb, Ben, Kij, Lane, and Amy for their support and encouragement. Shawn Casey for his technical knowledge (any mistakes are mine), and for loaning me his impressive collection of Chinese martial arts movies (which I will return, eventually). My agent, Sara Megibow, for her tireless work and wisdom. All the wonderful folks at Riptide for their enthusiasm and expertise. And Travis, for everything.

ALSO BY DON ALLMON

Blue Unicorn series
Apocalypse Alley (coming soon)
The Burning Magus (coming soon)

ABOUT THE AUTHOR

In his night job, Don Allmon writes science fiction, fantasy, and romance. In his day job, he's an IT drone. He holds a master of arts in English literature from the University of Kansas and wrote his thesis on the influence of royal hunting culture on medieval werewolf stories. He's a fan of role-playing games, both video and tabletop. He has lived all over from New York to San Francisco, but currently lives on the prairies of Kansas with many animals.

Connect with Don:

Website: www.donallmon.com

Twitter: @dallmon

Pinterest: pinterest.com/donallmon

Enjoy more stories like *The Glamour Thieves* at RiptidePublishing.com!

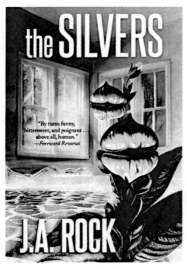

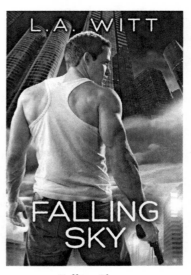

The Silvers
ISBN: 978-1-62649-432-9

Falling Sky:
The Complete Collection
ISBN: 978-1-62649-040-6

Earn Bonus Bucks!

Earn 1 Bonus Buck for each dollar you spend. Find out how at
RiptidePublishing.com/news/bonus-bucks.

Win Free Ebooks for a Year!

Pre-order coming soon titles directly through our site and you'll
receive one entry into a drawing for a chance to win free books for
a year! Get the details at RiptidePublishing.com/contests.

BCPL
Baltimore County
Public Library

CPSIA information can be obtained
at www.ICGtesting.com
Printed in the USA
LVOW07s1009190817
545584LV00001B/57/P

9 781626 496163